Helen D'Oyly Carte

Richard D'Oyly Carte

Arthur Sullivan

W.S. Gilbert

Helen D'Oyly Carte

Gilbert and Sullivan's 4th Partner

by Brian Jones

For Kathleen, Simon, Susan and Robert

Helen D'Oyly Carte
Gilbert and Sullivan's 4th partner

First published in 2011
by Basingstoke Books Ltd, 103 Rodenhurst Road, London SW4 8AF

Produced in England by 4word Ltd
Unit 15, Baker's Park, Cater Road, Bristol BS13 7TT

Contents

Worldwide Thanks

To the people at the British Library, their Newspaper Library at Colindale in North London and Westminster Library I owe a special debt of thanks. Not only did they come up with the goods, they continue to show me how to use the microfilm. Thanks also to the Pierpont Morgan Library in New York.

From the United States, David Stone, Don Smith, Ralph MacPhail and Hal Kanthor have been tremendous sources of information and encouragement. So have many of my Gilbert and Sullivan friends in the UK. These include Katie Barnes, John Cannon, Vincent Daniels, Paul Ernill, Peter Joslin, George Low, Peter Parker, Philip Plumb, Philip Walsh and Chris Webster.

'Savoynet' on the Internet makes it possible for enthusiasts worldwide to exchange Gilbert and Sullivan information. This too has been a rich treasure house.

I owe a particular debt of gratitude to Dame Bridget D'Oyly Carte, who was Helen's step granddaughter. She encouraged me to write this book in the first place.

My son Simon Jones carried out the indexing quickly and efficiently. It would have taken *ages* if I had done it myself.

The painter Walter Sickert was a friend of Helen and
Richard D'Oyly Carte.
His painting 'After the Rehearsal' is on the front cover.
His etching 'The Actor Manager' is reproduced above.

1

"Mr Carte, You need someone to tidy this office."

This is the story of Helen D'Oyly Carte. She was described as the fourth partner by D'Oyly Carte's long-serving principal comedian Henry Lytton[1]. He wrote:

> "So far I have given in this chapter the random reminiscences of the chief three figures – the triumvirate, as I have called them – at the Savoy. But there was also a fourth, and it would be a grave omission were I not to mention one who was, in my judgement, as wonderful as any of them. I refer to Miss Helen Lenoir who, after acting for some years as private secretary to Mr Carte, became his wife. There was hardly a department of this great enterprise which did not benefit, little though the wider public knew it, from Mrs Carte's remarkable genius. It was not alone that hers was the woman's hand that lent an added tastefulness to the dressing of the productions. She was a born business woman with an outstanding gift for organisation. No financial statement was too intricate for her, and no contract too abstruse. Once when I had to put one of her letters to me before my legal adviser, he declared firmly 'This letter <u>must</u> have been written by a solicitor.' He would not admit that any woman could draw up a document, so cleverly guarded with qualifications.
>
> Mrs Carte, besides her natural business talent, had fine artistic talent and was a fine judge, too, of the capabilities of those who came to the theatre in search of engagements."

1. *The Secrets of a Savoyard*, Henry Lytton. Jarrolds Publishers, 34 Paternoster Row, London EC4 pages 70–71

Helen first met Richard D'Oyly Carte on Monday 26 February 1877 at around 12 noon. Carte was working in the family firm, Rudall Carte. They had a fine reputation as flute makers. Richard D'Oyly Carte had already established himself as a concert and dramatic agent. Into his office walked a little lady in a fur-lined cloak. Her figure was slight, and she had big, dreamy, and depthful eyes. These eyes were sharp, alert and showed a very keen intelligence. She was confident, because she carried a note of recommendation from someone whose judgement, she knew, was valued by Carte[2]. She told him her name was Helen Lenoir, and she wanted work as an actress. But her interview with Carte did not go as she expected. "Oh no," Carte said. "All my actors are coming back from pantomimes and I cannot find places for any of them. And I am sorry, but I now have to go out to lunch. But at present I do not need anyone at all."

"Oh yes you do, Mr Carte," said Helen. "You need someone to tidy this office."

Carte went out to his luncheon appointment. When he came back, there in his tidied office he found Helen and a filing system.

My interest in Helen began in 1981 when I was editor of *The Savoyard* magazine for the D'Oyly Carte Company. I received an article from Paul Seeley who was the company's repetiteur (rehearsals manager) and the topic was 'Who was Helen Lenoir?' My reaction was a mixture of excitement and apprehension. This was a genuine scoop. However, the company continued to be run by Dame Bridget D'Oyly Carte. She was, after all, Helen's step granddaughter and I had no idea whether she would wish to have the article published.

Dame Bridget was delighted by the article. She liked and admired Helen. She told me that she met Helen only once. She was only five years old when Helen died. Dame Bridget remembered that Helen was already very ill when they met. She asked her Private Secretary Albert Truelove to provide background information to help in my search.

Dame Bridget gave me help in several ways. She told me that she had been approached by Charles Couper Dickson. Charles had gained a fine reputation throughout the world of aviation for his drawings of airplanes and liveries in the early days of Croydon Airport. Charles had also carried out research into the Couper and Black families from which he came and into which Helen was

---

2. The note of introduction came from Michael Gunn. He had been managing the Dublin theatre where Helen had appeared in pantomime. Full details are shown in chapter 4 of this book.

born. He has kindly passed his notes to me. These include a summary of what he had discovered about Helen and are dated November 1979. Dame Bridget was extremely delighted by the new information which Charles had provided. She wrote to him:

"I am full of admiration for the work you must have done, over many years, to collect so much material. It has always been difficult to answer the question my father had often been asked 'Why has there never been an adequate account published about Richard D'Oyly Carte and Helen?' Frankly he felt there were, as I believe you have clearly realised, really not enough facts based on and supported by written material, letters and so on, and personal knowledge to make such an account possible and sufficiently interesting to justify such a publication. It is sad that when relatives and friends were still alive there was apparently nobody willing or capable of the necessary research and of writing such an account."[3]

Dame Bridget's letter includes section about her enthusiasm for Wigtown, where Helen was born:

"Your account of her early life, coming as she did from Wigtown, as these last three or four years I have been making yearly visits to Galloway and have become very fond of this part of the world and have in fact been associated, with friends, with a little laird's tower so-called 'castle' where I have spent some time each year".

Charles also gave me a superb collection of 19th century family photographs[4] that had been collected by Helen's great grand niece, Miss Marjorie Andrew of South Australia. The picture of Helen with her sister Hilda and her elder brother John was published with Paul Seeley's article in *The Savoyard*. I am convinced that, already by this stage of their lives, Helen and John were showing signs of high intelligence. Other family photographs appear in the next chapter of this book. With Albert Truelove's help I started to learn more about the background of the D'Oyly Carte Company. I started to collect press articles from all over the

3. Letter from Dame Bridget dated 26 August 1980 from 1 Savoy Hill, London WC2. Author's collection.
4. Photographs of Helen's family are supplied by Charles Couper Dickson. They are now in the author's collection

United Kingdom and North America. Many of these will feature in later chapters.

Dame Bridget put me in touch with Marjorie Andrew. Marjorie, with Shirley Clissold, another of Helen's great grandnieces, had undertaken the task of publishing the diaries of Helen's brother, John McConnell Black. Deciphering the diaries was not easy at all as they were written in a variety of languages, including English, French and Pitman's shorthand. The diaries have now been published – in English all the way through.

A sheer stroke of luck provided me with a unique source of material about the family lives of Richard and Helen. In 1990 I took part in the first appearance on British TV of *The Sixty Four Thousand Dollar Question*. My subject was of course 'Gilbert and Sullivan'. Question master Bob Monkhouse asked me what I would do if I won the money. The answer I gave him was that I would visit the Gilbert and Sullivan collection in the Pierpont Library in New York. I did win the top prize, which was £6,400. So to New York I went.

When I arrived there, I found the array of objects rather hard to take in. The then curator Frederic Woodbridge Wilson came up with two Victorian volumes handsomely bound in leather. These turned out to be the diary of Richard's elder son Lucas D'Oyly Carte for the year 1888. I quickly realised that this was the year in which Richard married Helen. It included a day-by-day account of their family life and their rather unusual honeymoon.

A short paragraph in *The Era* adds an extra perspective on Helen's career:[5]

"Well do I remember the slight figure, the large, dreamy, depthful eyes of the little lady in a fur-lined cloak who came to D'Oyly Carte's agency offices in Craig's Court to get work of some kind. I happened to be with Carte when she called, and in my youthful insouciance took no particular notice of her. But D'Oyly Carte, with his Napoleonic estimate of individuals, was more discerning. 'That's a clever little girl, Desprez', he said. 'A very clever little girl.'"

Carte was to make much of Helen, and she was to make much of him.

An assessment of Helen's importance in the creation of the Savoy operas is to be found in the reminiscences of François (usually known as Frank) Cellier in partnership with Cunningham

---

5. *The Era*, 19 May 1913. Reference provided by the late Gerald Glynn

Bridgeman. The book was published in 1914 and Cellier died on 5 January 1914 so it is likely that Bridgeman wrote the following paragraph:[6]

"in the heart of that great enterprise there existed, unseen, a *Dea ex machina* – one feels tempted to say, over the destinies of the Savoy there presided a kind, gentle, ever-watchful spirit in the form of a woman whose wisdom, tact and energy did more to enhance the fortunes of the Savoy than the greater world can ever realise.

The woman was Mrs D'Oyly Carte...

It is confidently anticipated that the life-work of Helen Lenoir, wife of Richard D'Oyly Carte may yet form the subject of a separate volume. Than that no prouder or more powerful to a true woman's worth could be given to the world. It is only within the last twelve months that death released Mrs Carte from the managerial post which she had filled so faithfully and with such extraordinary skill and ability since the loss of her husband in 1901."

Well, you are right, Messrs Cellier and Bridgeman, to anticipate that Helen and her life-work will form the subject of a separate volume. It is almost a hundred years since you said so, but I have had a far wider range of sources than you had available when your book was published in 1914. My book tells the story of a remarkable woman, and she was an even more remarkable manager. I have enjoyed writing it. I hope that my readers will join me in enjoying her story.

6. *Gilbert, Sullivan and D'Oyly Carte* by Francois Cellier and Cunningham Bridgeman, Sir Isaac Pitman & Sons. London 1914. Pages 6–7

2

Helen's birth, childhood and early education

Much of the family information in this chapter comes directly from the biographical sketch that Charles Couper Dickson gave me in the late 1980s. He had taken this information directly from family records. He has also included information on the Coupers given to him by Sir Nicholas and Lady Couper. The earliest family member whom Charles has traced is Helen's great great grandfather George Couper who in the mid eighteenth century was living as a tenant farmer in Wigtownshire. All the people in this branch of the family wrote their names as Couper (not Cooper or Cowper). All family photographs have been supplied by Charles Couper Dickson and are now in the author's collection. Charles also traced a William Couper, Bishop of Galloway in the 17th century but could not prove any link to confirm the relationship with Helen's Coupers.

Helen was born at Wigtown on 12 May 1852. In the 19th century its main claim to fame was the tall obelisk which had been erected to serve as a Martyrs' Memorial. On 11 May 1685 Margaret Lachlan (Covenanter aged 63) and Margaret Wilson (Presbyterian aged 18) refused to take the Abjuration Oath whereby they accepted allegiance to the English Commonwealth. They were tied to a stake in the Solvay Firth and drowned when the tide came in.

Wigtown is a Scottish border town in the county of Galloway. Wigtown is near Scotland's west coast, and is about 100 miles south of Glasgow. It is a little way north of the English town of Carlisle. Today Wigtown has an international reputation as Scotland's Town of Books.

Helen's father was George Couper Black. He was a graduate of Edinburgh University. By the time of the 1851 census, he was procurator fiscal of Wigtown. This is the Scottish term for public prosecutor. However, there were few criminals to prosecute in the small peaceful town, so it was not a full-time job. George Couper Black managed the British Linen Bank. This bank had a proud history. George II founded it in 1746 by royal charter as the British Linen Company. All branches of the bank could carry on Linen Manufactory. Linen was a principal source of income for farmers and farm workers in the area.

Helen was born Susan Couper Black on 12 May 1852. Her sister Mathilda had used the name Hilda from early childhood, probably because she found Mathilda to be too much of a mouthful. Within the family Helen chose her name to match Hilda.

George Couper Black had a distinguished family background. One ancestor was the 18th century Scottish poet Dr Robert Couper. Helen's father's uncle was Sir George Couper, Comptroller of the Household of the Duchess of Kent (Queen Victoria's mother).

Charles Couper Dickson recalls his father saying to him: "My boy, you come from a long line of cattle-stealers" However, his family history shows that there was more than that to the Coupers. Helen's great uncle Sir George Couper had been knighted for his service to Wellington in the Peninsular War (1807–1814).

Wigtown in the 1850s was a very small town. At the time when Helen was born, the family lived in the Bank House. As the name implies, this was a tied house for the bank manager. Helen's family had to move to a smaller house in Main Street when her father George Couper Black died in 1863.

In the 19th century, travelling was part of a young gentleman's education. George Couper Black in turn visited Anglesey, Devon,

Southampton and Paris. In Devon he enjoyed the hospitality of a scholarly physician Dr Thomas Foster-Barham who lived at Castle Dyke, near Dawlish in South Devon.

Dr Foster-Barham was an ardent lover of all things classical Greek. He dressed in an Athenian style tunic. He wrote a Greek grammar. Originally he had intended to go into holy orders, but he found that he could not accept all the 39 articles. Instead, he became a doctor.

An early egalitarian, he suggested that large estates should be redistributed to the local peasantry, following the analogy of the French Revolution. As part of his egalitarian philosophy he insisted that his two servants sat and ate with the family at mealtimes. He encouraged free conversation by his 13 children during breakfast. His proviso was that the only language a child was allowed to speak was classical Greek. Presumably, the two servants also spoke and understood at least a little classical Greek.

George Couper Black wrote a number of letters to an aunt, describing his stay with Dr Foster-Barham. He did not mention any of the 13 children by name. However, five years later in 1850, he married one of the daughters, Ellen Foster-Barham. They married in the parish of St Thomas, Exeter. Helen's mother came from very far away from Wigtown. She was a Cornish girl.

One member of the Barham family was the novelist Hugh Walpole who in 1764 published The *Castle of Otranto*. This now recognised as the first Gothic novel. The initial 1764 edition was titled in full *The Castle of Otranto, a Story. Translated by William Marshal, Gent. From the Original Italian of Onuphrio Muralto, Canon of the Church of St. Nicholas at Otranto.* This first edition purported to be a translation based on a manuscript printed at Naples in 1529 and recently rediscovered in the library of "an ancient Catholic family in the north of England". The Italian manuscript's story, it was claimed, derived from a story still older, dating back perhaps as far as the Crusades. This Italian manuscript, along with alleged author 'Onuphrio Muralto', were Walpole's fictional creations, and 'William Marshal' his pseudonym. The 1764 edition is described as *A Gothic Story* on its front cover, Thus Walpole not only wrote the first Gothic novel, and he also created the name by which the genre was known. The genre has been rewritten, and parodied ever since. Jane Austen speaks well of the book in *Northanger Abbey*, in the second and subsequent editions.

Walpole acknowledges authorship of his work, writing "The favorable manner in which this little piece has been received by the public, calls upon the author to explain the grounds on which he composed it" as "an attempt to blend the two kinds of romance, the ancient and the modern. In the former all was imagination and improbability: in the latter, nature is always intended to be, and sometimes has been, copied with success."

REV. RICHARD HARRIS BARHAM
(THOMAS INGOLDSBY)

Another distinguished literary Barham was the Reverend Richard Harris Barham, who as Thomas Ingoldsby had published the *Ingoldsby Legends*. These are a collection of myths, legends, ghost stories and poetry supposedly written by Thomas Ingoldsby of Tappington Manor. It was actually a pen-name of the clergyman Richard Harris Barham. The legends were first printed during 1837 as a regular series of the magazine *Bentley's Miscellany* and later in *New Monthly Magazine*. The legends were illustrated by John Leech and George Cruikshank. They proved immensely popular and were compiled into books published during 1840, 1842 and 1847 by Richard Bentley. They remained popular during the 19th century but have since become little known. An omnibus edition was published during 1879 under the title *The Ingoldsby Legends; or Mirth and marvels*.

As a priest of the Chapel Royal, Barham was not troubled with strenuous duties and he had ample time to read and compose stories. Although based on real legends and mythology, such as the 'hand of glory', they are mostly deliberately humorous parodies or pastiches of medieval folklore and poetry. The most famous of these legends is 'The Jackdaw of Reims'.

When Richard Harris Barham was pursuing his undergraduate studies at my own college Brasenose in Oxford, he was rebuked by his tutor, Mr Hodson (later Master of the college). Barham was consistently absent from Morning Chapel at 7 a.m.

"The fact is", said Barham, "you are too late for me."

"Too late", said the tutor, in astonishment. "Yes sir," explained Barham. "I cannot sit up till seven o'clock in the morning. I am a man of regular habits and unless I get to bed by four or five at latest. I am really fit for nothing next day."

Among Barham's lesser known *Ingoldsby Legends* is 'Some Account of a New Play'. This describes the action of a 5-act melodrama which tells of romantic goings on among the nobility, with a dramatic sea voyage by moonlight and which ends with:

Moral
The public perhaps with a drama might quarrel
If deprived of all epilogue, prologue or moral
This may serve for all three then – Young Ladies of property
Let Lady A's history serve as a stopper t'ye
Don't wed with low people beneath your degree
And if you've a baby don't send it to sea
Young Noblemen, shun everything like a brawl
And be sure when you dine out or go to a ball
Don't take the best hat that you find in the hall
And leave one in its stead that's worth nothing at all!

Punsters in the 19th century, including Planché and even W.S. Gilbert would have enjoyed the rhyming of property and stopper t'ye. And the melodramatic touches that follow through from Walpole and Otranto all the way to *Ruddygore* and Mad Margaret seem to have been echoed in the creative, maternal line of Helen's family.

Barham died in 1854 and the *Memoir of the Reverend Richard Harris Barham* that his son wrote as an obituary sums up his character.

"Perhaps his virtues were of a kind especially adapted to win their own reward; certain it is, he had ever cause to view humanity under its fairest aspect. He never lost a friend: he never met with coldness or neglect. His family loved him devotedly; those upon whom he was instrumental in conferring benefits were rarely, if ever, wanting in gratitude: and his own claims to consideration were readily and liberally allowed. All these things pass away. As an author, he cannot be forgotten. His productions, whatever may be their defects or blemishes, must occupy that niche in the literature of the country, which his originality has carved out."

Barham, like W.S. Gilbert, found that his mind was at its clearest when other people were not there to interrupt. So there is a precedent within the Barham side of the family for Helen being able to work at all hours of the night and early morning. The other characteristic of the Barhams was that they understood and used the skills required in creative writing. Helen used these skills only occasionally in writing for the stage, but she was an absolute expert in letter-writing and even in cryptic telegrams.

When Helen's mother first came to what must have seemed to her the distant Scottish town of Wigtown, she found the life-style very different from that of Castle Dyke in Devon. Helen's brother John McConnell Black wrote: "My mother must often have felt herself in a strange land when she came as a bride to the British Linen Company's Bank, Wigtown." The gulf between England and Scotland was considerably deeper in the middle of the 19th century Scotland than ever it had been in the English county where she had been brought up.

Take the language or dialect, for instance. The 'lower classes' spoke it all day and even educated elderly folk would drop into it and say "Are ye gaan tae the Kirk?" and "What for no?" ("Why not?") There were novelties in the kitchen – the girdle – the iron dish hung over the fire for baking the cakes – oat cakes and parritch (porridge) not yet introduced into England. A lad threatening another (and usually smaller) lad would say "Ah'll gar you greet" ("I'll make you cry.")

John McConnell Black adds: "But her gentle ways and kindly speech soon won her all the affections of the Scottish lassies who offered freely for housework in those days. My mother told me in later years that the ordinary rate of pay was £3 a year and a new dress at Michaelmas." So that gives us a clear picture of the environment in which Helen was brought up.

Those who have seen the 1953 film *The Story of Gilbert and Sullivan* may recall that the actress playing Helen spoke with a marked Scottish accent. John McConnell Black and presumably Helen saw this as being the way the 'lower classes' spoke. John recalls an occasion when they went to visit the Foster-Barham family, who by the time had moved from Cornwall to Castle Dyke, Highwick, Devon. "We brought a servant girl and my mother had sometimes to act as an interpreter between her and the Devonians." Dr Foster-Barham left £500 in his will

(proven 1869) to Helen's mother with equal shares for her four children when they reached the age of 21.

During the lead-up to *Topsy-Turvy*, I was helping with the research. I repeatedly put my view to Rosie Chambers, Mike Leigh's researcher about this. I was pleased to see that the actress Wendy Nottingham, playing Helen in the film, avoided the pitfall of stage Scottish. Classical Greek was a permitted language in the Black household, but stage Scottish was not.

With Helen, none of the accounts or interviews that I have read gave the impression that she spoke in 'the guid Scots tongue'.

John McConnell Black was born on 28 April 1855. Helen's younger brother Alfred Barham Black was born on 7 October 1858. Helen's older sister Mathilda Sarah was born in on 21 January 1851[1]. I have left her till last in the list because that gives me the chance to clear up another common mistake. Most writers have said that Helen changed her name from Susan Couper Black to Helen Lenoir as a stage name. In fact the change to Helen took place much earlier. Mathilda Sarah was only ever known as Hilda, probably because she had difficulty in pronouncing the full Mathilda when she started to talk. Helen took her name because Hilda and Helen sounded well together (alliteration with a little assonance). Both Susan and Helen were names of great aunts in the Black family.

Wigtown was a small quiet town. The Black family was Presbyterian, but they were by no means as fiercely against the theatre as some of the other Scottish families of that time. John McConnell Black recalls some high spots for himself.

> "Sometimes a circus arrived, or a troupe of Christie Minstrels sang in the town hall. The notes of the Mocking Bird song remained in my mind for long years afterward. I found them more moving than the Scottish psalms sung in the parish church."

The 1861 census shows Helen, her parents and the other children living at Bank House. There are three domestic servants. There is also Miss Elizabeth E. Griffith, described as English Governess. Miss Griffith must have played an important part in Helen's early education. So must Helen's mother who, as we have seen, knew classical Greek. It is interesting that the three elder children are

---

1. Birth dates are as shown in the family tree compiled by Charles Couper Dickson. Paul Seeley found the day and month when Matilda Sarah (Hilda) was born in Wigtown parish and public records.

described in the census as Scholars, attending School. Matilda (Hilda) is shown as 10 years old. Susan (Helen) is 8 and John is 5. It was progressive of father, probably with mother's influence, to give good primary education to the two girls. The youngest child Alfred was two years old and so had not yet reached school age.

Charles Couper Dickson wrote:

"From earliest childhood Helen evinced great mental ability. She was to prove a most versatile young lady, a brilliant scholar and a fluent linguist. Though deceptively slight, fragile and delicately built, she had unbounded energy and determination, a clear intellect and a generous, compassionate nature. These qualities she may well have inherited or absorbed by precept and example from her mother, who has been described in very similar terms, and I think was like her in appearance. Helen's outstanding legal and business acumen and head for figures, for which she was to become famous, came perhaps from her lawyer cum banker father."

On 25 April 1863 Helen's father George Couper Black died of "liver disease and general anacarca". This was a swelling caused by the effusion of fluid into his body. So he would have known that his life was soon to end. He was able to leave adequate money to his widow and for his children's education. Helen's brother John McConnell Black went to Wigtown Grammar School in 1864. Helen and Hilda, as girls, had to depend on private education. It is likely that Miss Griffith continued to teach them.

In 1866 the family moved to a "rather uncomfortable" flat in King Street, Edinburgh. John went to Edinburgh Academy. He was bullied and labeled a 'cad'. This at the Academy meant that he lived in a flat, not a self-contained house. Helen and Hilda depended on private tuition.

On 3 March 1869 Helen's maternal grandfather died. Despite his egalitarian principles he was a wealthy man. His estate included sugar plantations in the West Indies. Helen's family moved to North Bristol, close to where the Barham family lived. Helen's mother was already suffering from tuberculosis, and the doctors advised her to live in a milder climate.

Helen's brother John McConnell Black kept a diary[2] which started in 1875. John had started his education at Wigtown

2. *The Diaries of John McConnell Black 1875–1931*, edited by Marjorie Andrew and Shirley Clissold.

Grammar School. He later went to Edinburgh Academy. When the family moved to South West England John attended Bristol Grammar School. He transferred to the Commercial School in Dresden in 1872. Helen and Hilda, as girls, depended on private education. Helen's younger brother Albert, born in 1858, went to Bristol Grammar School, and later to a grammar school in Taunton.

Although Helen and Hilda did not attend any school, John's reminiscences make it clear that their home life included a great deal of reading and discussion of the ideas in the books.

When he arrived in Australia in 1876, John McConnell Black had been trained to work as a banker or an accountant. He found these professions were at that time not easily accessible to entrants with a Scottish background. At the age of 22 he tried to make a living from farming at which he took a farm in Barotoa where he worked for three years but the droughts and the adverse economic conditions made farming unprofitable. He moved to Adelaide and got a job with a local newspaper *The Register*. He later transferred to *The South Australian Advertiser,* and this was the newspaper which published the interview with Helen which appears in Chapter 9 of this book. The interview was given to me by Charles Couper Dickson.

The flora and fauna of South Australia had been little recorded, even though there were some flowers and animals that were unknown in Europe and some that were unique to South Australia. John and his wife Alice cycled widely around the area, recording what they saw on every trip. John's formal study of botany began in 1900.

He meticulously kept diaries of his life, and these of course contain much botanical information. But it is John's letters to and from Helen that form the basis of much family information about how Helen's life developed.

3

Great diligence and proficiency at London University

On 11 May 1870, the day before Helen's 18th birthday, Queen Victoria opened the new buildings of London University. This was the first time that the university opened its doors to women. On 18 May 1871 *The Times* reported that Helen Susan Black was as the first of four successful women Honours candidates. With "private tuition" she had beaten girls from Cheltenham Ladies (Miss Beale) and North London Collegiate (Miss Buss). Helen had gained "the highest distinction in Higher Mathematics, Mechanics, Logic and Moral Philosophy". She showed "great diligence and proficiency in all her studies, and spoke several languages fluently."

A pupil at one of these eminent schools composed the comic but affectionate rhyme:

Miss Buss and Miss Beale
Cupid's darts do not feel
How different from us
Are Miss Beale and Miss Buss

Dorothea Beale was a pioneer in the struggle for women's education. She was among the first pupils to attend Queen's College when it opened in 1848. In November 1850 her mathematical tutor, the Reverend T. Cook gave Miss Beale a certificate of efficiency in Arithmetic, Geometry, Algebra and Trigonometry. His opinion was that "she has acquired a sound knowledge of the first principles of these four subjects showing considerable ingenuity in the application of them to examples and problems."[1] Before the end of 1871 University College conceded

1. *Dorothea Beale of Cheltenham.* Archibald Constable & Company, London 1906, pages 31–32

15

that women had the right to be "liberally educated" – and started to plan accordingly. "17 professors would teach their several subjects to students of either sex within the college walls with 'separate arrangements for separate classrooms'". The College Charter was to be revised to admit women to 24 classes but the Charter was not revised and the separate classrooms were not built.

Helen pursued her studies without distraction. On 13 June 1873 *The Times* reported that Helen Susan Black had recently passed the London University Examination for Women for Special Certificates of Higher Proficiency in Mathematics and Mechanical Philosophy. Mathematics enabled Helen to have a secure touch in managing the salaries of actors and actresses in the Carte companies. Mechanical Philosophy would nowadays be known as Technology. It related directly to the backstage management of electrical power, in which D'Oyly Carte was to lead the theatrical world.

In her third year Helen completed her studies at a higher level than she had taken in 1871. On 5 June 1874 *The Times* reported that Helen Susan Black had recently passed the London University Examination for Women for Special Certificates in Logic and Moral Philosophy. Logic and Moral Philosophy were to be useful to Helen when she had to negotiate, not least during the 'Carpet Quarrel' with W.S. Gilbert. She also had a good supply of charm.

Her brother John returned from Leipzig in 1876. He reached London on 25th October and joined the cashier's department of the Oriental Bank Corporation. By 12th November he was staying in a flat at 3 Carlisle Place, Victoria Street, London. This is a prestigious address, and is close to London's theatres, which in the 1870s were located in the Strand. It is unlikely that either Helen or John would have been able to afford a flat here on their own incomes.

John's diaries show that Helen's first year in paid employment was patchy and she was not committed to a career in education. She tried her hand at teaching as a governess. By May she was working with a friend, Miss Alice Grüner at 3 Carlisle Place, Victoria Street, London. It was through Miss Grüner's friendship that Helen and John were able to stay at Carlisle Place.

John records that in May 1876 his mother was staying at 3 Carlisle Place. Miss Grüner taught Russian to John (and presumably Helen). In July Miss Grüner went to Liverpool to teach three young ladies. Helen joined her there and they were still at Birkenhead on 15 August.

John reports that Hilda had "a fancy to go over to Rome." He met her in Paris at the convent of the *Dames Auxiliaires* in the Rue de la Tour d'Auvergne on 18th April 1876. John had been required to explain his presence through an iron grille on the outer door. He was then admitted to a room where he spent half an hour contemplating a portrait of Pope Pius XI. Hilda explained that she had been advised to go into the convent for religious instruction. However, her life had not become totally monastic, and John reports that Hilda was glad to go out with him on a visit to the *Bois de Boulogne.*

In December 1876 John reports that Helen was "not finding teaching satisfactory, she took lessons in elocution, dancing and singing." Luckily indeed for Gilbert and Sullivan followers, Helen had decided not to follow a career in teaching. She continued her religious life as a Presbyterian.

Couper family records show that Helen and John's mother Ellen had for some time suffered from 'chest complaints'. In 1877 Ellen decided that in search of a warmer climate the family would move to Melbourne in South Australia. In fact Helen's mother lived on until 6 July 1902 – a testament indeed to the beneficial South Australian climate. She tried very hard to persuade Helen to go with the rest of the children, but Helen determinedly refused.

The next chapter shows how Helen moved into a career to which she happily dedicated the rest of her life.

4

First steps in Helen's career

Helen's success in her studies at London University enabled her to earn a good living as a tutor to girls in well-off families. This is the career that she started on. In 1874, after her university studies, Helen went to live in London. She had made friends with a young lady student, Miss Grüner. They provided private tuition, sometimes in partnership, to cover different subjects. When Helen's brother John came back to London from Leipzig in 1875, he called to see Helen on his way home to Bristol. By 1876, the whole Black family had moved to London. In May 1876, John recorded that mother was staying with Helen and Miss Grüner at 3 Carlisle Place, Victoria Street. This was an upper-class part of London. Miss Grüner must have belonged to a well-to-do family. She greatly valued her friendship with Helen. Her family paid some of Helen's rent, or possibly did not charge any rent at all. Miss Grüner also taught Russian to Helen, John and their younger brother Albert. In July 1876 John reported that "Miss Grüner had gone to Liverpool to teach three young ladies". Helen joined her there. John records that Helen and Miss Grüner were still at Birkenhead on 15 August 1876.

Helen started to show an interest in the London theatre in 1875. John recalled in his *Memoirs* that he had seen both *Trial by Jury* and *The Happy Land*. He wrote that *The Happy Land* had a rather daring conception because it portrayed Gladstone on the stage. "The 'Grand Old Man' wore his typical collar with broad wings" and spoke with portentous gravity. It is likely that John talked to Helen about the two plays. Indeed Helen and her brother may have seen one or both of these plays together. *The Happy Land* opened at the Haymarket Theatre on 4 January 1873. It was in fact a parody of *The Wicked World* by W.S. Gilbert. The first night programme attributes it to F. Tomline and Gilbert à Beckett. A note on the programme says it is produced "with the special sanction by W.S. Gilbert". No wonder Gilbert granted his special sanction. F. Tomline was a pseudonym for none other than W.S. Gilbert.[1] *Trial by Jury* was of course the first opera of Gilbert and Sullivan that was managed by Richard D'Oyly Carte. But *The Wicked World* was managed by Marie Litton, and Richard D'Oyly Carte had nothing to do with it.

Although Helen was still working as a tutor in 1876, she had set her mind on a theatrical career. S.J. Adair Fitzgerald records: "With a view to preparing herself towards her new career she took lessons in singing, dancing and elocution," [2]

Helen got her first acting engagement before the end of 1876. In December, her brother John wrote that Helen had gone to Dublin. *The Era* magazine reported from the Theatre Royal, Dublin that *Aladdin and His Wonderful Lamp* opened on Tuesday 26 December with 'no little effect'.

A full-length report a week later said that the success of *Aladdin* "seems assured, and we should not be surprised were it to distance all its predecessors in popularity." In the seventh scene, the fair princess is wooed in turn by Prince Piccadilly (from London), Prince Pat McCoy (from Dublin), Prince Sandy McGregor (from Scotland) and Mr Washington Brick (from across the Atlantic). Helen played the part of Prince Piccadilly. Like the other four suitor princes, she did not succeed in persuading the fair princess to marry her. Helen was in the chorus for the other scenes. She used her dancing skills in Scene 5, the Ice Ballet. *The Era's* forecast of a long run for the pantomime was confirmed. The final performance of *Aladdin* was on Saturday February 24 1877.

Now Helen wanted work in London. She had made a useful contact in Dublin. The manager of the Theatre Royal, Dublin was Michael Gunn. Earlier in 1876, he had welcomed *Trial by Jury,* managed by Richard D'Oyly Carte, with whom he established a long-lasting, friendly and very successful business relationship. By the oddest coincidence, Michael Gunn and Richard D'Oyly Carte each introduced the other to their future wives. Bessie Sudlow (real name Barbara Elizabeth Johnstone and born in Liverpool in 1840) returned to her native England in 1875 after an

1. The Happy Land, Its true and remarkable history. Terence Rees. W.S. Gilbert Society Journal issue 8 1974
2. The Story of the Savoy Opera. S.J Adair Fitzgerald, Stanley Paul & Co, London 1924, pp 8–12

early career on the New York stage. From June to August 1876 she was principal soprano for Richard D'Oyly Carte's touring Opera Bouffe Company, appearing in Great Britain and Ireland as the Plaintiff in *Trial by Jury*, and Amanda in Carte's own *Happy Hampstead*, The tour was managed by Michael Gunn, who for a number of years was Carte's silent partner in financing the early Gilbert & Sullivan operas. Shortly after the tour Miss Sudlow became Mrs. Gunn and retired from the stage. Gunn later built and operated the Gaiety Theatre, Dublin. Upon his death in 1901 the ownership of the Gaiety passed to his widow who retained possession until 1909.

Carte was to benefit from Gunn's help, managerial and financial in the future. Gunn on at least one occasion took over the running of the office in London. He later became a director of the Savoy Hotel. So Helen had good reason to believe that a note from Michael Gunn would influence a London impresario and agent such as Richard D'Oyly Carte. Remarkably, the text of a similar note from Gunn to Carte in the late 1870s still survives. Gunn's nephew was George Edwards, later the manager of the Gaiety Theatre. Gunn sent Edwards to Carte's office with a note: "This is George Edwards. Give him a job, pay him a pound a week, and make sure he earns it." Carte gave Edwards a job in the Box Office of the Opéra Comique. George Edwards soon became George Edwardes, adding an e to give distinction to his name.

It is possible to work out precisely the day when Helen had her first meeting with Carte. *Aladdin* finished on Saturday 24 February. Helen crossed by steamer from Dublin to Liverpool on Sunday 25. She caught an early train at about 8.00 am from Liverpool to London on Monday 26 February 1877. That is why she reached Carte's office just before lunch time, never the ideal time to meet a manager. This is also when she first met Frank Desprez. He later became Editor of *The Era*, a valuable ally in publicity for Carte and Helen. In the first half of 1876, Desprez was working on the libretto of a one act musical farce *Happy Hampstead*. It was produced at the Royalty Theatre in Soho on 13 January 1877. The music was credited to Mark Lynne. This was a pseudonym for Richard D'Oyly Carte. Desprez wrote of Helen: "Her character exactly compensated for deficiencies in his. D'Oyly Carte was a man of ideas and impulse, of violent fits of work and ardent periods of enjoyment, and he was rather untidy, at any rate in his office." I acknowledge that Desprez says it was on the second or third visit that Miss Lenoir asked if she might be allowed to tidy the office. The scene I quoted in Chapter 1 was from *The Stage* obituary. I find it the more likely.

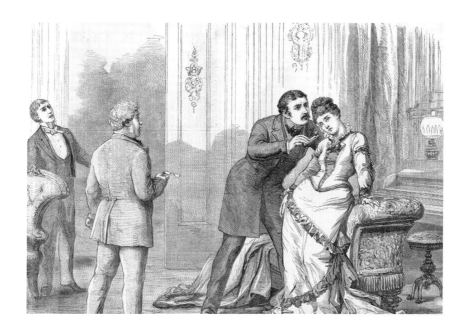

Every writer up to now has presented the picture of Helen committing herself to the organisation of D'Oyly Carte from that moment. This is not accurate. Helen's second stage appearance came on tour in a play entitled *The Great Divorce Case*. This premiered at London's Criterion Theatre on 15 April 1876. The actor manager was Charles Wyndham who was building a reputation for farcical comedy.

The writers were John Doe and Richard Roe. Both names are pseudonyms. John Doe's real name was Clement Scott, who became the first editor of *The Theatre*, launched in August 1878.[3] Scott (pictured here) remained a good friend of Richard and Helen throughout their lives. So Helen had already been associated with the future editors of *The Era* and *The Theatre*. The picture is taken from *The Illustrated London*

3.   The Illustrated Sporting and Dramatic News, London, 6 May 1876

News of 18 May 1876. *The Great Divorce Case* was enthusiastically reviewed.

The Great Divorce Case

Our predictions with regard to the new comedy at the Criterion Theatre have been verified. It is the success of the season. Since the first night the business has been greatly improved by Mr C. Wyndham's deft manipulation, and the

Woodbury Permanent Photograph.

long life of the comedy assured. The scene chosen for illustration by Mr Friston is one in which Mr Wyndham does <u>not</u> appear. It is where, after a series of *contretemps* at the hotel, in which the two barristers, who are recklessly out for the night, have ignominiously figured, the innocent victim of the Great Divorce Case flies to the succour of the lady, who has assumed a severe attack of indisposition in order to shield the then hidden cause of her distress. Miss Nelly Bromley, We shall 'treat' Mr Wyndham by-and-bye. Here is his carte de visite.

Of course, Miss Nelly Bromley had played the Plaintiff in Carte's first Gilbert and Sullivan success, *Trial by Jury* at the Royalty Theatre a year earlier. Musical theatre in London was in few but talented hands in the 1870s.

In spring 1877, a company touring *The Great Divorce Case* played the provinces. A playbill in the Theatre Museum gives details of a production at the Theatre Royal. Sauchiehall Street, Glasgow in March 1877. There is a full cast list. Helen Lenoir had the named part of Caroline. Helen is listed as having appeared at Theatre Royal, Dublin. Everyone else in the cast is credited as having appeared at a West End Theatre. A name that stands out is J.G. Taylor from the Gaiety Theatre. He was later to star as

Leonard Meryll in *The Yeomen of the Guard* and as Marco in *The Gondoliers* in D'Oyly Carte tours in the late 1890s. Taylor's presence must have been purely a coincidence. A programme of *The Great Divorce Case* in my own collection shows that by May 1877, Helen had been replaced in the role of Caroline. Helen must have received a persuasive SOS to come back and work with Carte in London. Meanwhile the whole Black family, all except Helen herself, had emigrated to South Australia in the summer of 1877. They hoped Helen would join them there. But John records that Helen found her true vocation "soon after we left England", i.e. in the summer of 1877. This summer was a very busy time in Carte's office. *The Sorcerer* premiered at the Opéra Comique on Saturday 17 November.

I saw a surprising letter in the Theatre Museum that her brother John and perhaps even Carte did not know about. A letter addressed to Helen Lenoir at 3 Carlisle Place, Victoria Street was returned to George Anderson Esq. She had signed up "as a Ballet Lady and to perform to the best of my skill and ability such utility characters on tour to Calcutta and India generally". The letter was returned after receipt of advance cheque and regrets. It was sent by Mr R. Blackmore of English's Dramatic Agency, Garrick Street. A note on the back of the letter signed by Blackmore says "This lady was engaged after Espinosa had seen her go through several steps." Another note on the back said "Weekly salary of Six Pounds Sterling." Espinosa had a high reputation as a dancer. He had written the standard work *The Elementary Technique of Operatic Dancing.* This was published by *The Dancer* magazine.

So, some time in late 1877, probably August, Helen had agreed to go as a Ballet Lady on a tour to Calcutta. Her salary in India would have been exactly four times as much as she was getting from Carte. Fortunately, Helen decided not to tour as a Ballet Lady in Calcutta. It is to the credit of Mr Blackmore and English's Dramatic Agency that they did not enforce the contract.

Life in Carte's office must have been very busy in the second half of 1877. Besides preparing the production of *The Sorcerer*, Carte's agency business of finding engagements for singers, musicians, and lecturing writers continued at full speed. In my own collection, I have a letter from Carte to the manager of the Brighton Aquarium. It is of particular interest because it is dated 16 June 1877, within the first two months of Helen coming back from her tour with the Wyndham company. The text is written in Helen's hand and signed by Helen, as from Richard D'Oyly Carte.

Dear Reeves Smith

The eminent Trumpet Soloist of the Royal Italian Opera Mr T Harper has two months of the summer at liberty. Carte adds that he will be happy for Mr Harper to appear for a week at the Brighton Hippodrome, Carte adds two possibilities for filling vacant dates in July. Miss Giulia Warwick, Prima Donna of Carl Rosa's Company for the Saturday, Miss Jessie Bond (real good contralto and very pretty) for a week

This letter shows the close links between the Carte's business as arranger of concert performers and the operas. Giulia Warwick created the mezzo soprano role of Constance in *The Sorcerer*. Jessie Bond joined the company to sing Hebe in *HMS Pinafore* in May 1878. She was indeed very pretty.

A letter in David Lovell's collection displayed in the Buxton Museum at the time of the 2010 Buxton Festival offers, with a degree of trepidation, another possible entertainer. It is dated 23 September 1878 and it is from 11 Beaufort Buildings, Strand, London SW

Dear Reeves-Smith,

I doubt whether you will give the terms Mr Stanley will require. I think we ought to give the *Spectre de la Rose* but you might let me know what you would offer

Le Spectre de la Rose is a ballet of the Ballets Russes based on a poem by Théophile Gautier. The music, by Carl Maria von Weber, was his 1819 piano piece *Invitation to the Dance*, in the 1841 orchestration by Hector Berlioz. Choreography was by Michel Fokine and set and costume design by Léon Bakst. It was later presented on 19 April 1911 by the Ballets Russes in the Théâtre de Monte Carlo. The story is about a debutante who falls asleep after her first ball. She dreams that she is dancing with the rose that she had been holding in her hand. Her dream ends when the rose escapes through the window. The dancers were Vaslav Nijinsky as the Rose and Tamara Karsavina as the Girl.

Arrangement of lecture engagements for H.M. Stanley was by no means a simple task. Sir Henry Morton Stanley, GCB (28 January 1841–10 May 1904), was born in Wales as John Rowlands. He became famous for his exploration of Africa and his search for David Livingstone. He is famed with saying to Livingstone on finding him where there were unlikely to be any other white men: "Dr. Livingstone, I presume?" This became one of the great catch-phrases of the day. Stanley's shyness meant that although he was eagerly received by his audiences he did not wish to become involved in conversation with them. He required that windows of his carriage on the trains to and from the speaking engagement were blacked out. Managing a tour by H.M. Stanley was a tricky business.

Greatly as Helen enjoyed the work with Carte, it was at this stage by no means certain that she would have a long-term future. Her brother John's diary has an entry dated 4 December 1877:

> "Today we received two letters from Helen and one from Aunt Mary. The first letter from Helen has been mislaid for 15 days.
>
> The letters have caused a lot of worry and upset our poor mother. In them Helen says that she is not able to leave her employment with Carte. (Confound the gods!) Furthermore the worst is that she has rented a house in Buckingham Palace Road for the mediocre sum of £70 per year. She had thought that the Misses Grüner would have joined with her in the rent. All this business has been as senseless as you could imagine. She also says that she is receiving regularly her salary from D'Oyly Carte, though I consider it a bit doubtful because in August she had written to me that there was no money in the office and now she is writing the opposite and only in October! Mother is going to write in the next mail that she should leave as soon as possible, after she has disposed of the house and the furniture. I will do the same."[4]

Clearly Helen's brother and her mother were doubtful about whether Helen's career was secure and had potential. But the letter from Helen in August 1877 about the lack of money in Carte's office clearly was an accurate description of his cash flow at that point.

---

4. *The diaries of John McConnell Black.* Volume 1 pages 60-61. Investigator Press. Hawthornden, South Australia

5

Richard D'Oyly Carte's family background

Helen D'Oyly Carte came from a fascinating family background. So did Richard D'Oyly Carte. His story is traced best by going back to his grandfather. The three generations involve grandfather Richard Cart (with no final e), father Richard Carte and Richard D'Oyly Carte, the founder of the D'Oyly Carte Company. The two later generations were Rupert D'Oyly Carte and Dame Bridget D'Oyly Carte.

The grandfather was born on 18 April 1787. He was the son of John and Mary Cart in St Mary's parish in Leicester. He started work on a farm, probably at the age of 10 or 11. Leicestershire is renowned as the birthplace of fox hunting. The county has some of England's most respected hunts such as the Belvoir Duke of Rutland's Hunt. Belvoir is pronounced beaver. Great grandfather John Cart may have had connections (or work) in the stables. Grandfather Richard Cart may have ridden the horses when their owners did not ride them – hence his horse-riding skill and connections with the upper class who might help him join the Royal Horse Guards (otherwise known as The Blues).

Leicestershire was famous for the skill of its fighting men in time of war. Britain renewed hostilities against France on 18 May 1803. Richard Cart joined the Royal Horse Guards at the age of 18. It is likely that a member of his employer's family had been commissioned into the Royal Horse Guards and Richard Cart went with him as the groom to care for his horse. The regiment provided board and lodging and his uniform, but his pay was very low.

Richard Cart was actively involved in the fighting. On 28 March 1809 he was promoted to the rank of corporal. His pay increased but it remained modest. He took part in Battle of Vittoria on 21

June 1813. He served throughout the Peninsular Campaign in Spain and Portugal from October 1813 to July 1814. He was posted to Flanders and participated in the so-called Hundred Days' War (it actually lasted for 111 days) from Napoleon's return from exile on Elba to Paris on 20 March 1815 and the second restoration of King Louis XVIII on 8 July 1815. Richard Cart took part in the Waterloo Campaign.

Richard Cart had met a young lady named Sarah Bartlett. On 28 March 1808 at Silchester in the county of Hampshire Sarah gave birth to a son, and this child was Richard Carte. Hampshire parish records show that Sarah Bartlett registered her child as base born i.e. illegitimate. Dame Bridget's record has the names of Hewlett and Shepherd written under this marriage, with a tick. William Sheppard (sic) married Sarah Bartlett of St Giles, Reading by licence at St Mary's Church, Reading on 5 June 1811. The variation of spelling between Shepherd and Sheppard does not indicate two different men. It is quite usual to find this sort of variation in family records at start of the 19th century. On 25 September 1812 Mary Ann Shepherd, daughter of William and Sarah Shepherd, was baptised at St Mary's Church, Reading.

So it is clear that Richard D'Oyly Carte's father was illegitimate. If this had become generally known, it could have had an adverse impact on Richard D'Oyly Carte's attempts to bring respectability to the English musical theatre.

For the first few years of Richard Carte's life, his father was on active service in Europe. Sarah Bartlett must have looked after Richard Carte, and it is clear that Richard Carte fitted well into William and Sarah's family. A piece of evidence that the good relationship endured is that Richard Carte acted as a witness when Mary Ann Shepherd married Charles Hollingsworth Hewett on 1 September 1840. Richard Carte signed his name with an e as witness to this wedding. The name Hewett is very close to Hewlett, which was shown on the Dame Bridget's record sheet. It may be that the confusion stems from whoever supplied her with the information.

As a young boy Richard Carte displayed great facility for picking up rudiments of instruments in his father's regimental band. The Colonel arranged for him to have piano and violin lessons from Professor Griesbach, member of the Royal Private Band. It seems likely that from 1808 until Richard Cart's marriage, Richard Carte lived with his mother. He lived near Reading and the band was based in London.

Grandfather Richard Cart married on 29 December 1820. Three sons were born to him and his wife Mary. The sons' names were George, Robert and Harry. Regimental records show Richard Cart was still non-commissioned at this time. Dame Bridget's record shows that Richard Cart's wife's name was Mary. Richard Carte may have moved from the Shepherd family and joined the Cart family at this point (i.e. when he was already 12 years old). Richard Cart received his commission in August 1823, His pay was still not huge – his half pay on retirement was 4 shillings (20p) per day. As a quartermaster he may have taken the opportunities to supplement his 8/- a day. This seems to be the only way he could have afforded his subsequent very affluent life-style.

Around 1826 Richard Carte had decided on the flute as his first instrument. He went to Germany to study under Herr Hauptmann, an outstanding flautist. When he came back to Britain Richard Carte added an e to his surname to avoid confusion with Britain's other top flautist Thomas Card.

Around 1830 Richard Cart retired from the Blues. He took to travelling abroad. At one stage, he was robbed of all his possessions. It was in the first year of Richard Cart's retirement that Richard Carte acted as a witness of the wedding of Mary Ann Shepherd to Charles Hollingsworth Hewett.

De Quincey's House
Soho
Fred Alcock

At the age of 43 (in 1830) Richard Cart decided to settle down. He secured an appointment as an adjutant of the Montgomeryshire Yeomanry Cavalry (a volunteer force of landowners, farmers and other townsmen). He lived in a handsome white Georgian house named Maesygarreg on the Gungrog Road in Welshpool[1].

In 1840 Richard Carte married Eliza Jones who was born in 1814 in Gower Street. Their home was in Greek Street at the heart of cosmopolitan Soho. They had five children. Their eldest child Richard D'Oyly Carte was born on 3 May 1844.

1. Land Registry/Cofestr Eiddo WA797260

28

Today Greek Street is famous for its splendid array of restaurants and little can be seen at street level of its distinguished literary and historical past. Originally Greek Street got its name from the church built nearby for Greek refugees. The church opened in 1677.

The actor, playwright and renowned conversationalist Douglas Jerrold lived in Greek Street. So did Sir Josiah Wedgwood and Sir Thomas Lawrence the brilliant portrait painter. The boy whom Thomas Gainsborough painted as 'The Blue Boy' was the son of Jonathan Buttall, hardware merchant in Greek Street.

Casanova stayed briefly in one of the lodgings in Greek Street in 1754. His periods of residence were rarely long-term. A legendary fictional resident of the street was Thackeray's Rebecca (Becky) Sharp in *Vanity Fair*.

A famous resident of Greek Street was Thomas De Quincy. In *Confessions of an Opium Eater* he describes his life as a feckless vagabond in a house where he was provided by with lodgings by a shady attorney who was one step ahead of the bailiffs. De Quincy's own description clearly identifies the house as the house where Richard D'Oyly Carte was born. De Quincy writes that it was situated on the north west corner of Greek Street, being the house on that side nearest to Soho Square'. This, in De Quincy's time, was numbered 58 but later re-numbered 61. It was structurally a subdivision of 27 Soho Square and originally the whole formed one large mansion which some time before 1790 was divided into two, and then at about 1794 both parts were largely rebuilt, though retaining dual character.

Richard Carte moved his family to London, presumably because there were more professional opportunities for a flautist in London than he was finding in Welshpool. But the house which overlooked Soho Square must have seemed to be a come-down, compared with the magnificent house and grounds in Welshpool. The date De Quincy gave for his occupation of the house was 15 August 1824. At that time the family in residence was that of Joseph Gandy, the architect. Visitors to London can see paintings by Gandy in the Pictures Room of Sir John Soane's Museum in Lincolns Inn Fields. Gandy lived there from 1812 to 1840.

What made the move to Greek Street even more of a come-down for the Carte family was that the house was multi-occupied. In 1842 Richard Carte 'professor of the flute' was listed as an occupant, but Robert Johnstone 'rising hinge maker' was also shown. However in 1844, when Richard D'Oyly Carte was born, Richard Carte was the sole occupant.

The house stood until 1938, when it was demolished to allow the building of the present numbers 27 and 28 Soho Square. De Quincy's connection with the site was commemorated with a tablet affixed by the London County Council in 1909. After demolition and re-erection of the building that became Nascreno House, the tablet vanished. Nascreno used the building for film production. It has now become an elegant Barclays Bank. I am grateful to Barclays because they sponsored me in my editorship of *The Savoyard*. I did not realise at the time the historical distinction of their Soho branch. The picture of Richard Carte was supplied to me by Terence Rees,

Richard D'Oyly Carte took the name D'Oyly from his mother's side of the family. Robert D'Oyly (a Norman Baron) built Oxford Castle in 1071. Today the castle has the reputation of being haunted. Eliza died in Hastings in 1885 and was buried in the nearby parish of Fairlight. Her husband Richard Carte was buried in the same grave. Richard D'Oyly Carte was buried in an adjacent plot in the Fairlight graveyard.

Richard D'Oyly Carte attended University College School in the 1850s. He developed a keen love of music and wanted to start as a professional musician. He left school to join his father's firm and study music in 1861 at age 17. He went on to compose and publish a number of his own songs and instrumental works. His musical compositions included two song sheets 'Stars of the Summer Night' dedicated to his sister Viola and 'Pourquoi?' dedicated to Selina Dolaro for whom he worked as manager in the early part of 1875[2]. The front cover says the song has *musique de D'Oyly Carte* and adds that it is published by Rudall Carte & Co.

Richard D'Oyly Carte's own opera, *Dr. Ambrosias, His Secret*, was first performed at St. George's Opera House in 1868, *Marie*

2. These songs were featured in David Lovell's exhibition 'A Company Promoter' at the Buxton Museum during the 2010 festival. The exhibition included the letter about Madame Ostoia, on loan from Peter Joslin who also loaned the letter from H.M. Stanley, quoted in this chapter.

performed at the Opéra Comique in 1871 and *Happy Hampstead* first performed at the Alexandra Theatre, Liverpool in 1876. He became lessee of the Opéra Comique on 5th June 1874. Throughout his life his ambition was to establish a vehicle for getting English Opera and Operetta on to the stage. However, Carte came to realise that his greater talent lay in management, and he soon launched a successful concert agency in Charing Cross. He managed Gounod's business affairs in England, and negotiated engagements and concert tours for Adelina Patti, the tenor Mario, and Edward Lloyd among others.

Peter Parker has kindly supplied me with some of Carte's lyrics for *Happy Hampstead*. Here is 'The Ginger Beer Song:

> Ginger Beer, so bright and clear
> Is the finest tipple going
> But quaff it pray without delay
> When once you set it flowing
> On plain or mount
> Its frothy fount
> The thirsty mortal blesses
> Pop pop pop pop
> Pray do not stop
> Drink while it effervesces

Perhaps this is a sign that Richard D'Oyly Carte had a brighter future as an impresario than as a librettist.

Richard D'Oyly Carte had a step-brother named Charles Hollingsworth Hewett who had been born at Reading on 20 April 1841. His father, also named Charles Hollingsworth Hewett, was the man who had married Mary Ann Shepherd in 1841 and at whose wedding Richard Carte had been a witness. He too had musical ambitions and a good baritone voice. He used his family connection with Richard D'Oyly Carte's burgeoning agency business to obtain singing engagements at concerts. Richard D'Oyly Carte helped him into the theatrical world. Hewett first appeared under D'Oyly Carte management in 1874 as the Footman in Andrew Halliday's farce *The Pretty Horsebreaker* and Prince Isidore in the comic opera *The Broken Branch* at the Opéra Comique. Pretty horsebreakers were the young ladies who trotted their horses along the fashionable Rotten Row in Hyde Park. Richard D'Oyly Carte had already formed his own light opera company presenting these works.

Richard Carte was a partner in the firm of Rudall, Rose and Carte & Company, music publishers and musical instrument makers. This was changed to Rudall, Carte & Company when Rose died.

Richard D'Oyly Carte left school to join his father's firm and study music in 1861 at age 17. He composed and published his own songs and instrumental works. His musical compositions included an opera, *Dr. Ambrosias, His Secret*, first performed at St. George's Opera House in 1868.

Brighton Aquarium was a venue for which Carte was arranging performers and lecturers. It was the first aquarium to be constructed in Britain. It was an innovative and imaginative building, designed by the famous pier engineer Eugenius Birch and opened to the public in 1872. In the course of the next ten years it featured royal visits, a roller skating rink and an 11,000 gallon fish tank, the largest in the world. Lectures, concerts and performances were its special attractions. The first manager of the Brighton Aquarium was George Reeves-Smith. He matched Helen in his meticulous keeping of records. Four letters to him from Richard D'Oyly Carte have been preserved.

A letter recommending a French soprano Mademoiselle Ostoia is dated 28 January 1873 and the letter heading is Rudall and Carte & Co, Opera and Concert Agents, Charing Cross. Charing Cross no longer exists as a street name; it was the western end of The Strand between Trafalgar Square and Charing Cross station.

Two letters dated 1877 in the author's collection show that Carte had, by then, established independently his own office. They have the printed letter heading R. D'Oyly Carte, Musical and Theatrical Agent 11 Beaufort Buildings, Strand, London SW. They show that Richard D'Oyly Carte was already independent from his father's firm.

A letter regarding a lecture by the services of the explorer Sir Henry Morton Stanley is written on 23 September 1878. It also shows that Richard D'Oyly Carte already has his eye on the recently reclaimed area of land on which he was to build the Savoy Theatre. I believe that this is the office in which the first meeting with Helen took place in February 1876. The other letter offers the singer Enrique with accompanying musicians. We shall examine the Enrique letter in more detail in Chapter 6. At around this time Carte moved to a large office block at 8 Craig's Court. This was off Whitehall, just around the corner from the office of where father and son had worked together.

Richard D'Oyly Carte managed Gounod's business affairs in England, and negotiated engagements and concert tours for Carlotta Patti, Adelina Patti, the tenor Mario, and Edward Lloyd among others. Carte also found baritone engagements (concerts and church music) for Charles Hollingsworth Hewett who was using the name John Hollingsworth. Both Hewett and Richard D'Oyly Carte had found it was difficult to make a living as musical performers. Instead of becoming a professional musician, Richard D'Oyly Carte went to work in his father's firm of musical instrument makers of Charing Cross. He wrote somewhat wistfully "Wiser counsels prevailed."

Hewett/Hollingsworth appeared under Richard D'Oyly Carte's management in 1874 as the Footman in the farce *The Pretty Horsebreaker* and Prince Isidore in the comic opera *The Broken Branch* at the Opéra Comique. *The Broken Branch*, an English version of Gaston Serpette's *La branche cassée*, starred Pauline Rita.

A major step forward in Richard D'Oyly Carte's career as an impresario came when he commissioned Gilbert and Sullivan to write *Trial by Jury*. It is interesting that he called on 'J. Hollingsworth' to create the part of Counsel for the Plaintiff for the first few months of the original production of *Trial by Jury* at London's Royalty Theatre beginning March 25 1875. *The Daily Telegraph* noted: "Mr Hollingsworth did good service as the Counsel"[3]. However Hewett/Hollingsworth left the cast in May 1875, and reportedly travelled to Milan where he trained at La Scala. Nothing is known of any subsequent musical career.

Hewett was uncle to two later D'Oyly Carte artists, Tessa and Jeffrey Snelson. It is to Richard D'Oyly Carte's credit that he sustained the family links with the Hewett/Hollingsworth family at a time when it would have been more prudent to keep these links quiet.

3. Allen, Reginald *First Night Gilbert and Sullivan*, Cardavon Press, Connecticut 1975, page 32

6

The team with theatrical talents and connections

Carte's office was small and untidy. Helen found three colleagues when she started work there. They were Frank Desprez and two young men named George Edwardes. Together this small team made an enormous contribution to the staging of the operas. Frank Desprez and a George Edwardes became giants of the musical theatre.

Let's start with Frank Desprez. He was born in Bristol on 9 February 1853. He was the eldest of the 11 children of Charles

Desprez, a French silversmith. He was educated at Cosham School, Wiltshire and spent three years in his teens in the U.S. State of Texas. He returned to Britain in 1875. His first piece written for the theatre shortly thereafter was an English adaptation of *La Fille de Madame Angot*. When this piece went on tour, Desprez wrote a supporting piece called *Happy Hampstead*. The name of the composer was given as Mark Lynne. This was a pseudonym for Richard D'Oyly Carte. Desprez was part of Carte's circle of close friends. He worked with Carte for many years as his secretary.

Throughout his career with Carte, Desprez remained active in musical theatre. His English version of La *Fille de Madame Angot* was played at the Royalty Theatre in 1875, shortly after the run of *Trial by Jury*. Desprez wrote the libretto for *Happy Hampstead*.

Desprez wrote the libretti for ten short works for D'Oyly Carte, most of which preceded the Gilbert and Sullivan operas at the Opéra Comique and later the Savoy Theatre. These were curtain raisers which had long runs with principal pieces, and they were played in London and on tour throughout Britain as forepieces, benefit pieces and short-programme items. Working with composers such as Alfred Cellier and Edward Solomon, Desprez became perhaps the most popular librettist of one-act operas in Britain. These included *After All* composer (Alfred Cellier 1878), *In the Sulks* (Alfred Cellier 1880), *Mock Turtles* (Eaton Fanning 1881) *A Private Wire* (composed by Alfred Cellier and co-written with Arnold Felix 1883), and *Mrs Jarramie's Genie* (Alfred and François Cellier 1888).

Desprez's most frequently played work was his 1879 two-act musical comedy, *Tita in Thibet*, which was later played in the British provinces by the Majilton company more than a thousand times. It was written as a vehicle for the music hall star Kate Santley. W. H. Seymour, who was to become the stage manager of the D'Oyly Carte Opera Company for 20 years, also played in the piece. The story concerns an unusual marriage custom purportedly to be found "in out of the way parts of the world" such as Tibet. The customs of the country permitted every wife to be simultaneously married to four husbands.

His best-known work, however, is a poem, *Lasca*, about a Mexican girl and her cowboy sweetheart caught in a cattle stampede "in Texas down by the Rio Grande." The ballad-like poem first appeared in a London magazine in 1882. It has often been reprinted, usually with deletions and changes, and recited in many parts of the English-speaking world. Between 1873 and 1882 at least four other of Desprez's poems had been published, two of which were about Texas.

Desprez collaborated with George Dance to write *The Nautch Girl, or, The Rajah of Chutneypore*. This "new and original Comic Opera" opened on 30 June 1891 and achieved a respectable total of 200 performances. It was one of several pieces that Richard and Helen brought in to fill the gap following the breakdown of the partnership between Gilbert, Sullivan and Richard D'Oyly Carte that was known as the Carpet Quarrel. Helen's influence in calming the quarrel is covered in Chapter 14. It included Gilbert and Sullivan performers Rutland Barrington, Rosina Brandram and John Le Hay. It then toured theatres in the UK provinces and overseas. *The Nautch Girl* significantly outran *The Vicar of Bray* (143 performances) and came close to *Haddon Hall* (204 performances). *Jane Annie or The Good Conduct Prize* was brought in while *Utopia Ltd* was being prepared and rehearsed. Its writers were J.M. Barrie and Sir Arthur Conan Doyle. Despite the eminence of these two names, *Jane Annie* limped rather than sprinted to its total of 50 performances.

In 1884, Desprez began writing for *The Era,* London's foremost theatre paper, and he became its editor in 1893, a position he held until illness forced him to retire in 1913. His position with *The Era* enabled him to recommend performers to audition for the Cartes. He wrote dozens of essays on travel, art, music, and famous personalities that were published in English periodicals, most of them between 1905 and 1913. Desprez died in London at the age of 63.

George Edwardes was born at the village of Clee near Cleethorpes, Lincolnshire, on 8 October 1855. He was the son of James Edwards, comptroller of customs. The family was Roman Catholic, originally from Wexford, Ireland. They had no direct link with the theatre. Indeed his father decided that George should train to join the Army. However, to join as commissioned officer rather than an ordinary private soldier, George needed to pass an examination. But he failed it. George[1] had moved to London and was living in Bloomsbury.

MR. GEORGE EDWARDES.

The glamour and the energy of the London theatrical world appealed to him. George had two cousins, John and Michael Gunn, who were managers of theatres in Dublin. Michael was Manager of the Gaiety Theatre. He was the man who had given Helen her part in the Aladdin pantomime.

Quite by chance, George met Michael Gunn when each was taking a lonesome stroll along the Strand, then the

1. Illustration of Edwardes from *The Play* volume 1 number 2 page 50

absolute centre of theatrical life in London. Michael had already made friends with Richard D'Oyly Carte. When George asked Michael for advice about what he should do, Michael suggested the theatre. George asked Michael for an introduction to help him in the theatrical world. Michael came up with a brief but effective note to Carte: "This is George Edwards. Give him a job, pay him a pound a week and see that he earns it". He initialed it MG. Carte immediately hired Edwardes as his Box Office Manager at the Opéra Comique.

It was a total coincidence that Carte and Edwardes both had an extra e added to the end of their names. Edwardes added his e shortly after he joined Carte – Michael Gunn had used the Edwards spelling when he wrote his recommendation to Carte. The e in Richard D'Oyly Carte had been added by his father, who wanted to distinguish himself from another Richard Cart who was already established as a musical performer.

Very shortly after Helen joined Carte, Michael Gunn had an additional reason for enthusiasm. From June to August 1876 the beautiful and talented soprano Bessie Sudlow appeared at the Gaiety Theatre in Carte's touring Opera Bouffe Company. She played the Plaintiff in *Trial by Jury*, Amanda in *Happy Hampstead* and Lange in *La Fille de Madame Angot*. Shortly after the tour Miss Bessie Sudlow became Mrs Michael Gunn and retired from the stage.

As we shall see in Chapter 12 Mr and Mrs Gunn became good friends of Richard D'Oyly Carte and Helen. The Gunns appear no fewer than seven times in that chapter.

With two young men named George Edwardes on Carte's staff it was found awkward at the Savoy to have two George Edwardes-es in the building and so the young manager in the office became Edwardes 'minor' and the one in the box office became Edwardes major, now Gaiety George.[2]

Edwards minor also had a distinguished career in the London theatre. In September 1899 he took over the management of Daly's Theatre from Augustin Daly, for whom the theatre had been built. He continued as manager until October 1915. He was succeeded by his daughter, Mrs Dorothy Julia Gwynne Sherbrooke (née Edwards).[3]

In 1885, Edwardes major succeeded John Hollingshead as manager at the Gaiety Theatre, producing the burlesques in which the Gaiety specialized. In 1886, Hollingshead retired, and from

2.   The Music Box by James M Glover. *The Stage*, London 5 May 1913, page 23
3.   *London Theatres and Music Halls 1850-1950* by Diana Howard. Library Association London WC1 1970

then on the Guv'nor (as George Edwardes came to be known) was in charge, with the assistance of the theatre's star player, Nellie Farren. She had entered the Gilbert and Sullivan story even earlier than Carte because one of her earliest claims to fame was that in Gilbert and Sullivan's first opera *Thespis* she played Mercury, the shop steward of the gods. It was her comical task to present their complaints. The next show that Edwardes produced at the Gaiety was *Dorothy* (1886), a comic opera similar to the Gilbert and Sullivan operas produced for Carte. *Dorothy* was a spectacular success. It starred the former Gilbert and Sullivan performers John Le Hay and Marion Hood, who was in the title role. The libretto was by B. C. Stephenson. The music was by Alfred Cellier who had been number 2 choirboy to Sullivan's number 1 when they were at the Chapel Royal. Cellier had also been Musical Director for Carte at the Opéra Comique. He took over from G. B. Allen in *The Sorcerer*, and conducted the early performances of *H.M.S Pinafore*.

Unfortunately for Edwardes he decided after a few months that *Dorothy* did not have much of a future. He sold the rights to his accountant Henry Leslie. Leslie's revised production clocked up 931 performances. It became the longest-running piece in musical theatre history up to that time. It significantly outran *The Mikado* (672 performances).

Edwardes continued his Gilbertian links He produced Gilbert's *His Excellency* at the Lyric Theatre. This opera, with libretto by Gilbert and music by Frank Osmond Carr, was first performed on 27 October 1894. Its cast included such familiar faces from the Savoy as George Grossmith, George Griffenfeld, Governor of Elsinore, a practical joker, Rutland Barrington (as the Regent), and Jessie Bond. The cast also included Nancy McIntosh, the American actress whom Gilbert had 'adopted' as his daughter. Most reviews praised Gilbert's libretto, but Carr's music was less well thought of and the opera closed after 162 performances.

7

Secretary in London, emergency in Paignton

Helen took over the secretarial work when she joined Carte's team in February 1877. At that point, the income to the office came solely from Carte's activities as booking agent for speakers and performers. One regular and very important customer was George Reeves-Smith. He became Manager of Brighton Aquarium when it opened in 1872. Carte immediately realized the scope for concerts and lectures by the singers and famous personalities he was representing.

When Helen came back to Carte's office in autumn 1877, she must have been excited by the new technology involved. As we saw in Chapter 6, Carte was already trusting Helen to carry out responsibilities. Here is the full letter from 11 Beaufort Buildings dated 23 October 1877.[1]

> G Reeves Smith Esq
> Dear Sir
> <u>Enrique Tour</u>
> Dear Sir
> In reply to yours – what offer can you make me for the party?
> R D'Oyly Carte

At the base of the letter is the figure of 20 gns (i.e. guineas). This is presumably the amount that Reeves-Smith had decided to offer. Directly below Carte's name are the initials: HL.

Just six months after she joined Carte's office he already trusted Helen Lenoir to write and sign letters on his behalf'.

---

1. This letter is in the author's collection.

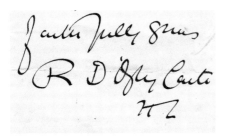

However Helen had not by any means committed herself to a long career with Carte.

A letter addressed to Helen Lenoir at 3 Carlisle Place, Victoria Street was returned to George Anderson Esq. She had signed up "as a Ballet Lady and to perform to the best of my skill and ability such utility characters on tour to Calcutta and India generally". The letter was returned after receipt of advance cheque and regrets. It was sent by Mr R. Blackmore of English's Dramatic Agency, Garrick Street. A note on the back of the letter signed by Blackmore says "This lady was engaged after Espinosa had seen her go through several steps." Another note on the back said "Weekly salary of Six Pounds Sterling." Léon Espinosa was a dancer famed throughout Europe. Born in The Hague and trained in the Paris Ballet School, he quickly won a high reputation in Paris. He moved to London in 1872 where he specifically practised and trained others in operatic dancing. Dancing was to become a significant skill for the D'Oyly Carte artists. It was fortunate indeed that Helen changed her mind about becoming a Ballet Lady in India. It is to the credit of Mr Blackmore and English's dramatic agency that they did not attempt to enforce the contract. If Mr Blackmore had insisted, Helen would have been obliged to sail to India as a Ballet Lady on a tour to Calcutta. At £6 her salary in India would have been four times as much as her salary with Carte.

As mentioned in Chapter Four Helen's brother had written of the family's doubts about the stability of the company. There is no mention in John's diary that Carte was about to launch *The Sorcerer* on 17 November 1877. *Trial by Jury* in 1875 had won Carte an enthusiastic following, so it may be that cash for advanced bookings was coming into Carte's office in October. Certainly there was plenty of work for Helen in the rest of the year. Soon after the launch of *The Sorcerer* in London, the first touring company went out on the road. They started with a matinee at the Opéra Comique on 9 March 1878, and the first provincial opening was in Liverpool on 11 March. They did 5 weeks in Scotland and two in Dublin. The tour lasted in total for 22 weeks, covering main towns like Manchester, Birmingham, Nottingham and Leeds and Liverpool. Helen helped out with railway bookings for cast and scenery, records of auditions and much of the general administrative work.

HMS Pinafore was launched at the Opéra Comique on 25 May 1878 and the first tour opened in Bradford on 9 September. The response was enormous, both in London and on tour in Britain. It was equally huge in the United States, and the lack of an international copyright agreement meant that there was no protection for the writer's and composer's rights. The first 'pirate' production in the United States was at the Boston Museum on 25 November 1878. This was precisely six months after the London opening. In total there were 150 'pirate' productions in North America. W. S. Gilbert was especially incensed,[2] not only because of the lack of

royalties, but because of the very poor theatrical standards of the 'pirate' companies cashing in on their own interpretations of *HMS Pinafore*.

Helen played an important part in achieving copyright protection for *The Pirates of Penzance*.

Relatively late in their quest for copyright protection of *The Pirates of Penzance*, they realized that they should not leave their new opera unguarded in Britain. The way to do this was to arrange a performance in the seaside town of Paignton by an English touring company. Mr D'Oyly Carte's First *Pinafore* Company had disbanded in Bristol on 13 December 1879. So, by a process of elimination, it was Mr D'Oyly Carte's Second *Pinafore* Company that gave a single performance in the Royal Bijou Theatre on 30 December 1879.

The Second Company had some people who were performing at a high standard. Richard Mansfield played General Stanley. Following the death of his mother in 1882, Mansfield went to the United States and achieved a highly successful career there. Fred Billington played the Pirate King. He became an absolute stalwart of the touring companies, continuing until his death in 1917. The contralto Fanny Harrison played Ruth. She had joined the Second *Pinafore* Company only in the month before the copyright

---

2. Paper presented by Colin Prestige at International Conference, Kansas University, May 1950, 'D'Oyly Carte and the Pirates', published by University of Kansas Libraries pages 115–119

performance. She continued as a D'Oyly Carte touring contralto until 1890.

The company needed a stage director who understood the D'Oyly Carte ethos and who would be undeterred by the difficulties involved in the production. Although there had not been time to ship the finished full score back to England, the Paignton performance had to be of a high standard. Helen was chosen by Carte to be the director because he knew she appreciated the importance of the situation and he knew he could rely on her. She had time for only one rehearsal, which took place after the scheduled Monday night performance. The cast rehearsed *The Pirates of Penzance* after performing *HMS Pinafore*. It must have been well after midnight before they could go home.

On the following afternoon they performed in the Royal Bijou Theatre in the Gerston Hotel in nearby Paignton. It had a small auditorium with room for about 50 people. A plaque commemorating the performance is on the Hyde Road side of the hotel. In the early 1980s, just before the original theatre was demolished, I looked around it and clambered into the loft where I could inspect the original ornate mountings of the theatre. Small as the Bijou was, class distinction ruled strictly in the allocation of the seats. The best seats were designated as 'sofa stalls' and cost five shillings (25p in decimal currency; the 'second seats' were two shillings the 'area' was one shilling and the gallery was six pence (2½ pence). Helen realised that upper class audiences were willing to pay for a privilege.[3]

Arthur Hyde Dendy's 'gem of a theatre' was a few miles away from the Lyceum Theatre (sometimes called the Assembly Rooms) in Abbey Road, Torquay where Carte's Second *Pinafore* Company was performing *HMS Pinafore* for the first time in the provinces.

It was directly due to the pirating of Pinafore that *The Pirates of Penzance* came to be staged for the first time in Devon. That first performance was to secure copyright and played the day before the first performance in New York.[4]

So while the principal soloists were in New York rehearsing *The Pirates of Penzance* for its premiere performance on 30 December 1879, Helen was trusted to stage the opera for the first time in Britain, a day before the American performance. She thus secured the British copyright.

The opera was completed in the United States and sent piecemeal to England. Miss Lenoir brought her touring company

3. Gilbert and Sullivan a dual biography, Michael Ainger, Oxford University Press, New York 2002, p 18
4. Centenary Souvenir Booklet, The Gilbert and Sullivan Society, Torbay branch

to Torquay for the Christmas season 1879 and the only chance of squeezing in one performance of the new opera was to hire another theatre for a matinee. Monday 29 December at 2.00 pm was quickly negotiated with Mr Dendy at the Bijou, and advertised in the *Paignton Gazette*, published on Saturday 27 December. However, the first pages of music had not been received in London and the performance was postponed until the same time on 30 December.

The music arrived in Torquay from London on 29 December, to give the Pinafore company only one rehearsal of the completed piece. They would have known most of act one and something of act two. The rehearsal took place on stage at the Lyceum Theatre, Torquay, immediately after the Monday performance of *HMS Pinafore*.

Helen's production was well received by the one critic who attended the performance. *The Paignton and Newton Directory* of 31 December 1879 concluded with the judgement: "We are sorry that time does not permit of our giving more than the above meager description of the story, which is exceedingly funny, and of the music we can speak in the highest praise. The airs are catching, and the concerted pieces are well worthy of our most popular English composer (Mr. Arthur Sullivan). We congratulate the talented author and composer on another brilliant success."

8

Manager in the United States

The potential for success and popularity of the Gilbert and Sullivan operas in the United States had been established clearly within a year from the first appearance of *Trial by Jury* at London's Royalty Theatre on 25 March 1875.[1] Its first performance in the United States took place at the Arch Street Theater in Philadelphia on 22 October 1875. Its first New York production was on 15 November 1875 at the Eagle Theater. This newly built theatre had opened only five weeks before the *Trial by Jury* premiere. The Eagle already had its regular company of actors and these were the people who played the parts in *Trial by Jury*. For example, the Learned Judge was G. H. McDermott. He never again appeared in any Gilbert and Sullivan opera.

However, Gilbert Hastings McDermott did have one very special claim to fame. He was renowned for his music hall singing of the ultimate patriotic ballad 'We don't want to fight but by jingo if we do'. This song had audiences jumping up from their seats. It generated its own word – jingoism. The *Trial by Jury* productions in Philadelphia and New York were, of course, long before Helen met Richard D'Oyly Carte or had obtained any job anywhere in a theatre.

The Sorcerer (premiered on 17 November 1877 at the Opéra Comique in London) was D'Oyly Carte's first ever full-length opera. However it was not produced in New York.

The success of *HMS Pinafore* (premiered on 25 May 1878 at the Opéra Comique in London) was totally unexpected and came in

---

1. Paper presented by Colin Prestige at International Conference, Kansas University, May 1950, 'D'Oyly Carte and the Pirates', published by University of Kansas Libraries pages 113–139

total contrast. In 1878, copyright protection for works originated in London was inadequate. The first pirate production was at the Boston Museum on 25 November 1878, six months after the London first night.

The fame of *HMS Pinafore* spread fast. *The American Review* made the following comment on 19 May 1879:

> "It is probable that Messrs Sullivan and Gilbert have builded better than they knew. They could hardly have anticipated so widespread and overwhelming a success for their merry little operetta. But its blended fun and intimacy have proved irresistible to American audiences who take their entertainment, as they do their food, from clean vessels. And it is not improbable that this comparatively unimportant work may be the means of starting the great work of regeneration of the modern stage in our native land. Clergymen have approved it. Church choirs have sung it. Church members have gone to see it and have been conscious of no moral degradation in the act."

The higher and more ethical the gathering, the more likely it was that piracy would strike. It was reported that a clergyman, speaking of the departed at a funeral service, said "We shall miss him very much". A female relative added "and so will his sisters and his cousins and his aunts."

The Bush Theater in San Francisco opened *HMS Pinafore* on 23 December 1878, just in time for Christmas.

The city of Philadelphia had strong Quaker and anti-theatrical traditions. The first performance of *HMS Pinafore* in Philadelphia took place on 6 January 1879. Two more Philadelphia theaters were playing *HMS Pinafore* within two months.

By the end of 1879, more than 150 American companies, from coast to coast, were profiting by many thousands of dollars from their pirate productions. There was one manager who behaved honorably. John Thompson Ford, writing from Baltimore, sent Sullivan a voluntary donation of £100 "as an acknowledgement of your authorship". Sullivan, appreciating that he had no legal claim to his own opera in the United States, hailed Ford's payment and politely described him as 'not one man in a hundred but one of a hundred and fifty American managers'.

By the end of 1879 two productions of *HMS Pinafore* authorized by D'Oyly Carte had taken place in New York. The production at the Standard Theater on 15 January 1879 closely matched the production of *Trial by Jury* at the Eagle Theater in November

1875. In contrast, the cast of *HMS Pinafore* at the Fifth Avenue Theater on 1 December 1879 was packed with star D'Oyly Carte performers. Jessie Bond as Hebe and Alice Barnett as Little Buttercup both repeated their Opéra Comique roles. J. H. Ryley had played Sir Joseph Porter in D'Oyly Carte's Comedy-Opera Company, the first touring company. The casting of Blanche Roosevelt as Josephine was a further clue. As Mlle. Rosavella, she made her singing debut at the Royal Italian Opera House, Covent Garden in 1876. She played Violetta in *La Traviata.* She was recruited to sing Mabel in *The Pirates of Penzance* when it opened at the Fifth Avenue Theatre at the end of December 1878. Her role in *La Traviata* meant that Sullivan could be confident that he had a soprano who would be comfortable with the high notes in 'Poor wandering one'.

One other notable performer appeared on 1 December at the Fifth Avenue Theatre. He was in the sailors' crew, and he wore a large beard to hide his true identity. His name was W. S. Gilbert. Gilbert later appeared in some of his non-D'Oyly Carte plays such as *Rosencrantz and Guildenstern*, but 1 December 1879 is the only known example where Gilbert appeared in a performance of one of his D'Oyly Carte operas.

Gilbert and Sullivan had been at the first out of town performance at the Broadway Theater, Philadelphia on 9 February 1880. They sailed back to England on 3 March to prepare for the English premier production at the Opéra Comique on 3 April. Helen sailed to New York a month earlier. She had been appointed to manage Carte's business in North America. She had her own office in New York, but she could still be called back to London whenever necessary. By Christmas 1882, she had commuted to New York no fewer than 13 times.[2] She took the United States to her heart, and the United States developed a similar affection for Helen.

Helen was the right person in the right place at the right time because she was aware of contemporary tastes. The next opera after *The Pirates of Penzance* was *Patience.* Much of the humour in *Patience* depends on the audience's understanding the aesthetic movement in Britain. The New York first night at the Standard Theater was on 22 September 1881, five months after the opening in London. An American theater historian Arthur Brown claimed

---

2. The Music Box by James M Glover, *The Stage*, London 5 May 1913, page 23. *The Green Room Book*, edited by John Parker, T. Sealey Clark Fleet Street, London 1909 gives figure 15 times before Helen's marriage. Helen's visits to New York for *The Mikado* (1885) and *Ruddygore* (1887) must be deducted.

that *Patience* was the greatest financial success that the Standard Theater had ever known, taking about 100,000 dollars. However, audiences in more far-flung parts of the United States were not as aware of the aesthetic movement as New Yorkers. Other books claim that Oscar Wilde was Carte's 'sandwich man' for the launch of *Patience* in the United States. In fact Wilde arrived in New York four days <u>after</u> the 100th performance at the Standard Theater. His long hair and aesthetic costume made Wilde the target of many cartoons and caricatures. There was no protection from unauthorized use in advertisements. Here he is advertising Red-Hot Cast Iron stoves.

OSCAR WILDE ON OUR CAST-IRON STOVES.
Another American Institution sat down on.

Helen enjoyed a good relationship with the United States press, because she had appointed Colonel W. F. Morse as her 'responsible agent.' She provided him with his own desk in Carte's office at 1267 Broadway. It was Colonel Morse who made contact with Oscar Wilde to agree his lecture tour. On 30 September 1882 Wilde received a cable: 'Responsible agent seeks to enquire if you will consider offer made by letter for 50 readings beginning 1st November. This is confidential. Answer.' Wilde responded with equal brevity on the following day. 'Yes if offer good.'

Morse also acted as responsible agent in arranging press interviews for Helen. She was tremendously newsworthy, not only because of her special position in the theatrical world but because she was also a stylish, attractive young <u>woman</u>.

Here is an interview which appeared in the *Philadelphia Times* on Monday morning, 16 May 1881. Helen is headlined as A SMART WOMAN who is business manager and right-hand man to D'Oyly Carte. The report says that most men who successfully manage opera companies are six foot high and weigh <u>two</u> hundred pounds. Instead, the reporter found "a girl as slight as Sarah Bernhardt and several inches shorter and looking to be about 18 years old." The physical description of Helen is fascinating:

> "Active without being nervous, bright, with large dark eyes that are never quiet, a face so mobile that it expresses her thoughts before she has time to speak them, small shapely hands that must have something to do even when their owner is at leisure, Miss Lenoir is the very incarnation of intelligent industry."

"Story?" she laughingly echoed in response to the reporter's request for the history of her life. "I haven't any. I am simply a girl who never could endure to lounge about indoors and fold my hands – that is all."

"But," persisted the reporter, "something unusual must have placed you in a position which many a man covets."

"Something? Well, I don't know what it was, except me." And now comes a lovely piece of invention to explain the exotic name Helen Lenoir. "I was born at Nice in the south of France – a lovely old place, and as stupid as it is lovely." She goes on to say that she went to London to teach French. She passed an examination at London University and after that had no difficulty in obtaining pupils. "But the work soon became very tiresome, not because of the quantity but the unendurable sameness. Then I decided to go on the stage."

"With no training?" asked the reporter.

"Only what I had given myself. Managers did not come in crowds to engage me, but having begun I resolved not to give up. At last I got an engagement and to go – where do you suppose?"

"Ireland? America?" suggested the reporter.

"Worse – a great deal worse. I contracted to go to India. The pay was not enormous. But I consoled myself with the thought that I would at least see a new country, and many things strange and curious. But the manager changed his plans and I got a small part on the London stage. There was nothing in it but the salary. Then one day I heard that Mr Carte needed an assistant."

"And you applied for the position?"

"Yes. It sounds ridiculous, doesn't it, for I was barely 17 years old then. Perhaps if I had been older, I should have been less confident, but anyhow I got the place and have held it ever since."

In the 1880s, misleading the gentlemen of the press was a fair and popular game. There is a lot of invention in Helen's answers. Yet what she says about her motivations and attitudes is precisely true.

The interview concludes with a section headed A WOMAN'S WORK.

"Isn't your work very exacting?"

The little woman shrugged her shoulders and burst into laughter. "Really, I don't know," said she. "I've never thought to ask myself that question. I only know that the work entirely agrees with me. I keep my health and spirits, generally keep my temper and am happier, I am sure, than ladies who have nothing to do."

"What are your special duties?"

Before answering Miss Lenoir looked suggestively across at her desk, on which lay an open cheque book, a pile of bills, a route list and several pieces of music. Finally she said.

"Well I cast all of our pieces. I select the players, the soloists as well as the choruses and assign them their parts."

"Then you must be an accomplished musician?"

"No, but I have a quick ear, and a true one. I can play at sight the accompaniment of any song that an applicant wishes to sing to show his or her ability and range and voice, and I don't think I have made many mistakes."

When Helen first arrived in New York, one of her first priorities was to enforce copyright for *The Pirates of Penzance*. The fact that the opera had already been premiered in New York did not by any means deter the would-be pirates. Here are the recollections of M. B. Leavitt, a man well-known in the New York theatre, first for his long career in theatre management and later as a theatre historian.[3]

"At a later date, Sydney Rosenfeld, then little known as a stage writer, obtained his first chance to make a name for himself by writing to my order a series of travesties of Gilbert and Sullivan musical pieces for the theatre. The Rosenfeld works burlesqued, in a light and graceful way, the notable features of the original operas. These pieces I produced with full scenery and costumes, employing leading artists, and the performances achieved much popularity.

One of the most successful of these, *Penn's Aunts among the Pirates*, was naturally talked about and invited the attention of D'Oyly Carte (then here with one of his companies) who had the impression that we were infringing his rights, and without announcement he came one evening to see for himself, and was so greatly pleased with the

3. 50 years in Theatrical Management 1859-1909, M.B. Leavitt, Broadway Publishing Co, New York 1912, page 398

manner in which the travesty was presented that he became profuse in his compliments, and willingly granted permission for me to make use of any or all of his operas in a similar way.

Carte's private secretary was Helen Lenoir, an English girl of great business ability for her years, and I may say, without seeming to be a pro-suffragist, that she excelled many men in this particular. Mr Carte valued her association in his affairs, not alone in its commercial aspect, but also for her high worth in what is best in womanhood, a condition later confirmed by their marriage.

D'Oyly Carte (when a boy) wrote an opera which has a public hearing in London. He began business as a concert and opera agent, and took singers of renown on several tours. Among these were Carlotta Patti and Signor Mario whose farewell tour he managed in the early Seventies. He was manager for Madame Dolaro during her London season when *Trial by Jury* was produced.

When Miss Lenoir joined Mr Carte's office force in 1877 he had no capital and it was not easy to get any for his scheme, nor to get a theatre, but he finally overcame all difficulties, and *The Sorcerer* was the first of a brilliant series which he produced at the Opéra Comique.

Mrs Carte has said in all probability the Gilbert and Sullivan partnership would have ended with *Pinafore* had it not been for the enormous American success of that work. The next opera, *The Pirates of Penzance*, was first produced in New York, Mr Carte coming here for that purpose, the author and composer accompanying him.

After its presentation at the Fifth Avenue Theatre, four *Pirates* companies were formed for tours under Mrs Carte's direction. She certainly at that time was not more than 20. In a letter I received from the lady, she said:

'I shall never forget my anxiety and nervousness when I started in February 1880 on the old Cunarder *Gallia* for (to me) an unknown country of whose geography I was ignorant, and soon after I found myself alone with four tours to book and three hundred artists to manage; but it had to be done and as youth is always hopeful, I did it'.

Mrs Carte expressed to me a liking for her experiences in the States. The managers were courteous and business-like, and she had no trouble with any of them. Among them were Haverly, Stetson, Hooley, Daly, Tomkins and Abbey. She was not only concerned with the Gilbert and Sullivan operas, but handled the productions of *Billee Taylor, Olivette* and several others."

Here is the performance history of the New York debuts of D'Oyly Carte premier productions. *Patience* opened at the Standard Theater on 23 September 1881. It ran for 177 performances. Helen managed the production and arranged Oscar Wilde's tour to the United States.

Iolanthe opened at the Standard Theater on 25 November 1882, the same day as the premiere in London and had 80 to 90 performances, Helen managed it. *Princess Ida* opened at the Fifth Avenue Theater on 14 February 1884, and ran for six weeks until 22

March. It was directed by Savoy actor Frank Thornton, A revised production in New York in November 1884 ran for only three weeks.

The outstanding success was *The Mikado*, which opened at the Fifth Avenue Theater on 19 August 1885 and achieved the magnificent total of 250 performances when it closed on 17 April 1886. A series of trade cards featuring D'Oyly Carte actors in their roles in The Mikado quickly found their way to New York and far beyond. The card shown features George Thorne as Ko-Ko.

No subsequent opera came anywhere near the success of *The Mikado. Ruddygore* (1886) had only 45 performances. *The Yeomen of the Guard* (1888–9) closed after 100 performances. *The Gondoliers* (1890) despite changes of cast and theater, lasted only from 7 January to19 April. With a high percentage of New Yorkers of Italian origin and New York's liking for grand opera, *The Gondoliers* could have expected a good long run, but it did not happen. *Utopia Limited* ran for 6 weeks in 1893.

9

An Australian interview that is close to home

I have quoted press interviews with Helen throughout her career. One interview is so special that it is worth quoting in full. It appeared in *The South Australian Advertiser* on 4 August 1885

INTERVIEW WITH A THEATICAL MANAGERESS

"One of the passengers by the *HMS Paramatta* was Miss Helen Lenoir who has for several years past managed an important part of the ever-extending business of Mr R. D'Oyly Carte, the well-known owner and manager of the Savoy Theatre, London in the theatrical and playgoing world. Mr Carte's name is already associated with Messrs Gilbert and Sullivan's, all in which he has been the means of introducing to the public. Nothing could give a better idea of Miss Lenoir's position and business capacity than the following remarks made by Mr Carte himself in a recent London interview: 'No account of my administrative work would be complete without reference to Miss Helen Lenoir, the young lady who has entire direction of the provincial and American business. Without her invaluable assistance I could not possibly have conducted the numerous enterprises I have had in hand. Miss Lenoir began some years ago by undertaking certain correspondence for me, but I soon discovered in her a remarkable business aptitude – an aptitude which, as far as my experience goes, is unprecedented in a woman. She has a wonderful perception, energy, and administrative ability, and, to crown all, the power to govern others. Miss Lenoir is better known in New York than in London. For four winters, unaided except by letters and cablegrams by me, she superintended all my undertakings in America. The achievement was nothing less than a sensation in that go-ahead country.

Miss Lenoir has acquired a tolerable knowledge of law generally, and can draw up an 'ironclad' agreement as well as any solicitor. On international copyright and dramatic rights she is probably one of the best living authorities; her knowledge is derived from practical litigation as well as text books. Before she came to me Miss Lenoir had passed with honours examinations at the University of London that would have entitled her to a BA degree had it then been given to women. Her industry and determination are positively appalling to weaker mortals'.

In the quest of news interesting to the readers of *The Advertiser*, a reporter waited on Miss Lenoir, to whom she kindly gave information on matters connecting with the operatic stage and lecturing platform. Judging from her youthful appearance one would not at first glance think that Miss Lenoir was weighted with the heavy responsibilities which she holds. She has so frequently undergone the severe ordeal of American interviewing that the milder antipodean article has no terrors for her. The next question asked was with regard to the latest operatic production of Sir Arthur Sullivan and Mr Gilbert, which Australians will soon have an opportunity to see.

The Mikado said Miss Lenoir 'was produced at the Savoy on March 14 of this year. The scene of the opera is laid by Mr Gilbert some hundred years before the discovery of Japan by Europeans, and in order to make the costumes conform as far as possible with the date of the play, we went to great trouble in obtaining designs and dresses worn in the Far East some two or three hundred years ago. In fact, we ransacked the principal Japanese warehouses in London and Paris, whose proprietors also imported numbers of dresses and curios necessary for the proper mounting of the piece. At the time the opera was in the course of preparation it so happened that the Japanese

Exhibition in Knightsbridge was going on, and we had the Japanese dancing master present at several of the rehearsals to teach the ladies of the company the rhythmical movements of the body and the wonderful fanplay which constitute Japanese dancing. Several of the young ladies from the Japanese village came to see the rehearsals and found great amusement in teaching our actresses how to imitate the walk. Or rather waddle, upon the high wooden shoes which are worn in Japan, *The Mikado* is one of the most expensive of the Gilbert & Sullivan operas, the dresses and scenery as produced at the Savoy coming to some £3000. In London *The Mikado* has drawn the largest houses of any of the operas, and has been considered one of the prettiest and most novel effects in colouring, dresses and scenery contributing mutually to this end. It has been well termed 'an idealised Japan'. Mr D'Oyly Carte has made arrangements with Mr Williamson, of Williamson Garner and Musgrove, for the production of *The Mikado* this year in Australia, and we are sending out costumes to him, which will be exact replicas of those in which the piece is now being presented at the Savoy. I am at present on my way to New York to bring out *The Mikado* in that city, and I know great excitement exists there in expectation of its production. Immediately on my arrival in Adelaide I received a telegram from England stating that an enterprising manager in America had attempted to infringe the right of production, and that we had obtained an injunction to prevent his doing so.

Theatrical Piracy
"You suffer a great deal from the attack of pirates who are less scrupulous in their dealings than those of Penzance!"

"Yes we are frequently engaged in lawsuits in America with managers who pirate our operas, in consequence of the want of an international law of copyright between England and the United States. Even at home we sometimes have to bring actions against amateurs, who persist in representing Gilbert and Sullivan's operas in the country towns of England without permission. Just before I left England we had a case of this sort against some amateurs who had pirated *Patience* in Nottingham, and, although the local sympathies of the intelligent jury had induced them to give a verdict for the defendants in direct opposition to the judge's charge and the weight of evidence, we ultimately won. The registrar of court declared the verdict a perverse one, and the judge ordered a new trial, whereupon the defendants asked that judgement might be recorded against them in spite of the decision of the jury. In fact, they were so sure of losing that they arranged for a charity ball in the town hall the same evening to defray legal expenses, to which, by the bye, they kindly invited me, although I felt obliged to decline."

"One of my actions is still pending, and threatens to remain so for an indefinite period. Some years ago, after *Pirates* was produced in New York, but before it was published, several American musical publishers wrote waltzes, quadrilles, etc from the airs of the opera and entitled them *Recollections from The Pirates of Penzance*. I obtained injunctions to restrain them all, but one very persistent German publisher of Philadelphia appealed to the higher court, the learned judges of which have been giving the case their consideration ever since, that is to say for some six years. Shortly after the appeal the opera itself was published, and of course anyone in America was at liberty to reprint the music. As any further fighting was of no interest to either party I offered to withdraw the case, but the publisher refused and when he died some twelve months ago he left strict injunction with his executors to carry on to the bitter end. When that will be no-one knows, and my lawyer tells me the case bids fair to rival the celebrated Jarndyce v Jarndyce."

How the companies are run
"How did the extensions of Mr Carte's business in America come about?"

"No sooner had *Pinafore* – the first of the series – appeared in England – then nearly one hundred companies began playing it all over the States. Some of the American managers realised fortunes from the piece, while the author and composer did not get a cent for their creation as far as the States were concerned. By-the-bye, some transatlantic manager did send £100 to Sir Arthur Sullivan and on the strength of that contribution he has since pirated several of the later operas. Seeing the immense success of *Pinafore* Mr Carte induced Gilbert and Sullivan to go there the following year and bring out *The Pirates of Penzance*. On the last day of 1879 the piece was produced at the Fifth-avenue Theatre for the first time in the world, without reckoning a small trial performance which we gave in the tiny seaside town of Paignton in Devonshire, one day before the New York debut, in order to secure the English copyright. *Pirates* proved an enormous success in New York, and we played it with five different companies at once, located as follows – New York, Philadelphia, north western states and Canada, New Orleans and the South, San Francisco and the Pacific Shore. I remained in America from the production of the *Pirates* to the following August, managing the entire business connected with these companies, and have since done the same with regard to *Patience* and *Iolanthe*. That did not necessitate so much travelling as you might think, as I managed most of the business from New York. My plan was to run down suddenly now and then to see how the travelling companies were getting on; in fact to drop upon them at unexpected moments, so as to see for myself how the operas were being played, and that there was no 'gagging' being done. In the London office we receive weekly over 600 letters concerned with Mr Carte's enterprises, and with my share of the correspondence alone I have two shorthand writers employed. It is the same in New York."

The Savoy
As regards their text, Mr Gilbert and Sir Arthur Sullivan are exceedingly particular. They insist that no alterations shall be made in words or music without their consent. Each new piece which we bring out at the Savoy is rehearsed with the utmost care under the personal inspection of the author and the composer for several weeks before production. Mr Gilbert arranged every detail of the stage business and takes vast trouble in seeing that his instructions are carried out. Private telephones communicate with the houses of both from the stage, so that they can hear the whole performance without personal attendance at the theatre. The Savoy is lighted with electricity, both on stage and in the auditorium, and was the first public building entirely so lighted. The satisfactory result is that while in gaslit theatres the heat of the highest point above the stage – technically known as the 'gridiron' – ranges from 100° to 150°, at the Savoy the temperature in that part only averages about 68°. The gallery is as cool as any part of the house."

The English companies
"In England we usually have five or six companies travelling in the provinces, including one composed of children. Oh no. these young interpreters of English opera do not have a hard time of it at all, and are passionately attached to their work. They have played *Pinafore* and *Pirates* with great success in London and the country. While travelling with us they are placed in charge of a number of properly qualified matrons and male caretakers, who see to their comfort. A schoolmaster travels with the company, and gives them lessons in the morning, and the performances are over in time for them to be in bed at the latest by half past 10. The little prima donna gets £5 a week, and the youthful Major General or Sir Joseph Porter nearly as much, besides board and expenses.

The children are as happy as the day is long and the only tears shed are when the tour is coming to an end. The worst punishment possible to inflict on any one of them would be to say "you can't play tonight." The management of these half dozen English companies keeps me full occupied during the summer. During the winter – the American theatrical season – I am generally in New York."

"Have you much trouble with the management of your artistes?"

"No, as a general thing they give me no trouble at all. Sometimes, however, it happens that an English actor who has made his debut in America, and does not understand the ways of the country becomes rather spoiled by praise and gets what is known locally as 'a swelled head'. Little difficulties arise in such cases."

Lecturing celebrities

"I believe you have arranged the lecturing tours of several European celebrities?

"Yes, acting for Mr Carte I arranged Mr Archibald Forbes's[1] first lecturing tour in England, and later in the United States and Canada. I also arranged Mr H. M. Stanley's first tour in England after his return from African exploration. There was a tremendous demand for him at the time, more particularly among the Y.M.C. Associations, where his lecture on 'The Dark Continent' was in great request. Mr Stanley is a man who personally dislikes publicity of any sort. At the railway-stations his constant efforts were directed to getting away without attracting a crowd. He would make at once for his carriage and draw the blinds down. As a lecturer he commanded higher prices than any other for whom we acted in England

Mr Bret Harte, the American humorist also lectured in England under our management. Until interested in the subject on which he is speaking his manner is very quiet, although he can say extremely smart things when he likes. On the platform he was not a great success, his excellent lectures being marred by being not quite audible in a large hall. He is now, I believe, American consul for one of the large European cities, and lives principally in London.

Mr Matthew Arnold is the most recent lecturer for whom we made arrangements in the States. His frequently expressed views that the minority is always right, and the majority wrong, and that

1. Archibald Forbes was a famous correspondent who reported the Franco Prussian War and British campaigns in Serbia, Turkey and India.

the salvation of a nation always depends upon whether the saving minority is strong enough to effect it, were, I should fancy, scarcely calculated to find favor with a democratic community. I don't know whether he felt quite sure that there was a sufficient 'saving minority' in the States to pull the republic through. Among the intellectual classes his addresses were an undoubted success."

"Did you make the business arrangements for any other celebrities in America?"

"Yes, Oscar Wilde, among others. His lectures and appearance made a great success in America. It became the fashion with a number of ladies to follow him about, very much in the same way as the aesthetic maidens follow Bunthorne in the opera. They used to throng rapturously round him at receptions; I remember on one such occasion a lady approach him, with clasped hands, exclaiming 'Oh, Mr Wilde, this is what I have longed for.' During his stay in America sunflowers became quite the rage, and ladies wore them everywhere in public."

"Is the general idea that Oscar Wilde was the original of Bunthorne correct?"

"As a matter of fact, Bunthorne's personal appearance on stage was modeled on Mr J. McNeill Whistler, the well-known painter and etcher, whose original opinions on art keep him constantly at feud with the Academicians. He is the owner of the celebrated white lock in the centre of the forehead which is the distinctive mark of Bunthorne. In Mr Whistler the effect is striking, because the rest of his hair is black. He is the author of such modern artistic terms as 'a nocturne', 'a symphony in black and grey', etc. Mr Oscar Wilde and Mr Whistler meet a great deal in the upper circles of London society and outvie one another in the production of witticisms, and Mr Wilde is sometimes accused of retailing his rival's good things as his own. At a large party not long ago, Mr Whistler achieved some bon mot before an admiring audience, and Mr Wilde, who was lolling a on couch close by could not help exclaiming – 'I wish I had said that.' Turning towards the rival aesthete Whistler replied – 'Never mind, Oscar, you will.' Mr Whistler also makes his debut as an art lecturer next year. He lately gave a brilliant lecture on that subject to a fashionable audience in London. He would not hear of his remarks being called a 'lecture', but entitled them 'his 10 o'clock'. Oscar Wilde always appeared before his American audiences in the celebrated knee-breeches, black silk stockings, and pumps. When the interviewers descended upon him on his first arrival, and asked him for his opinion about America and the voyage across he replied that 'he was disappointed with the Atlantic.' This was duly cabled over to the English papers, and as the passage had been a rough one it created some astonishment. Since his tour he has married a charming American lady, and he is not doing much beyond writing for the magazines and some of the newspapers.

Mrs Langtry and Miss Fortescue

"Was Mrs Langtry a success in America?"

"Yes, she had enormous success there. Of course, people had different opinions about her acting, but there was only one opinion about her beauty and grace of manner. Both she and Mr Irving and Miss Terry were successful in America, and took away a large amount of dollars with them. I believe Mrs Langtry would be a big attraction in Australia. As in America, all the ladies would want to see her, if only from curiosity, and probably a good many gentlemen too. Her charm lies less in regularity of feature than in her sympathetic voice and fascinating presence."

"Was not Miss Fortescue a member of Mr Carte's company in London?"

"Her first engagement on the stage was with us at the Savoy, where she played Lady Ella in *Patience*. She was a lady by birth, but her father had lost a lot of money, so that she was obliged to work to support herself and her mother.

She was gifted with a good voice and very attractive appearance. It was while playing in *Patience* and *Iolanthe* that she became engaged to Lord Garmoyle, and she threw up a very good position at his wish. Since she has recovered the £10,000 damages for his breach of promise of marriage she has been starring in the English provinces as Galatea. I believe she intends going to America, and possibly Australia, and there is little doubt that her beauty and the celebrity she has attained will draw."[2]

2. This rare autographed photograph is from the collection of George Low.

Australian business

"Have you business to transact in Australia?"

"As regards myself I am travelling to America via South Australia, in order to visit relatives in this country. I have been charmed by your city, and its numerous public and other buildings, which would do credit to a much older town. The Botanical Gardens I think especially lovely, and the unrivalled clearness of the air gives a particular beauty to the landscape, which I have never seen equaled in any other country. In Melbourne I am going to see Mr Williamson, and give him the prompt book and band parts of *The Mikado*, and arrange with him the details of the production. When Mr Williamson was in London lately he obtained from Mr D'Oyly Carte the sole right of producing all the Gilbert and Sullivan operas in Australasia for a considerable period. I have just heard from him that he will produce *The Mikado* at Christmas, probably in Sydney."[3]

John McConnell Black recorded Helen's visit in a diary entry dated 9 August 1885

> Dear Helen has come and gone. She arrived in the colony by the *RMS Paramata* at Glenelg about the middle of July and she sailed by the SS Adelaide for Melbourne yesterday (Sunday) she will pick up Miss Williams, the relative of Mr D'Oyly Carte, who is travelling round the world with her and they will go together to Sydney, taking the boat to San Francisco hence on 13 August. In my book of newspaper extracts is an interview which I had with her in which I gleaned a number of exciting particulars about her work in England and America and the story of how numerous companies are 'run'. We did our best to make her stay

3. J. C. Williamson produced *The Mikado*'s first authorised performance In Australia on 14 November 1885 at the Theatre Royal, Sydney,

agreeable. Of course, what she most longed for was living up at Burnside with Mother.

I took her and Miss Williams to Parliament House immediately on their arrival, also to the Public Library, Museum etc and the Botanic Gardens, also to the theatre where we saw Rignold and Miss Kate Bishop in *Called Back* – rather stale for both of them I fear.[4]

Helen was between times nearly going overland to Melbourne but, ultimately, relinquishing the idea owing to the night journey to Kingston and also the great difference in the expense – about £10 as against £4. It was certainly a pity that she could not reap more benefit from her long journey, attendant expenses, than a visit all in one month, but she hopes to return next year and pay us a longer visit. I only hope she will be able to carry the idea out.

4. *The Diaries of John McConnell Black*, Vol 1, Investigator Press, South Australia, page 232

10

Managing the companies on the road

On 3 March 1880 W. S. Gilbert and Arthur Sullivan sailed back to England on the *SS Gallia*. Richard D'Oyly Carte returned to England a week later on the *City of Chester*. He was tired but happy after his hard work. *The Pirates of Penzance* had established his claim to copyright in the United States. The Gilbert and Sullivan operas had won many friends in the New World.

There was an immediate need and an opportunity for someone to manage Carte's business interests in the United States. Helen was the ideal person. She immediately went out to New York. She just missed the first D'Oyly Carte production of *H.M.S. Pinafore* in the capital city. This had been a notable success in terms of the publicity it generated. Performers known to the London audiences played the lead roles. J. H. Ryley played Sir Joseph. Alice Barnett was Little Buttercup. Jessie Bond was Hebe, and Blanche Roosevelt sang soprano as Josephine. There was one other London notable

Photo by Marc Gambier, New York

on the stage that night. W.S. Gilbert, disguised by a large beard, was in the chorus as one of the sailor men.

D'Oyly Carte's production of *The Pirates of Penzance* in New York opened on 31 December 1879. Helen had managed the copyright performance two days earlier. She went straight from Paignton to New York, and arrived a few days after the New York opening. The box office receipts were tremendous. It was reported that Gilbert and Sullivan each received 400 dollars a week at the start of the run.

Helen had to manage the five Carte companies touring the United States and Canada. She came back to England in August 1880. She returned to North America each year until 1884.

An unusual tribute came from the touring companies on 19 May 1881. Two companies combined to put on a benefit performance on that evening. Helen won their hearts because of the successful publicity she provided, and her mathematical ability to make the journey from theatre to theatre smooth and rapid.

The Australian actress Kate Girard had performed leading roles in the legitimate theatre in New York during the latter half of the 1870s. She appeared in the chorus with one of two D'Oyly Carte and E. E. Rice Opera Companies playing *Billee Taylor* in America in the spring of 1881. Her name appears in the programme for Helen's benefit matinee put on by the combined companies in New York for Helen on 19 May 1881. The programme consisted of the first act of *The Pirates of Penzance*, the second act of *H.M.S. Pinafore*, followed by the first act of *Billee Taylor*. Miss Girard played Ruth and Little Buttercup in the first two segments

Audiences, managers and even the critics loved her in New York. Her combination of shrewd business judgement, seemingly inexhaustible energy and feminine charm won many minds and hearts. New York had never seen anyone like Helen before. The commonest cliché was 'D'Oyly Carte's' right hand man'.

A contemporary interview shows Helen's impact in 1881.[1]

The other smart woman alluded to is Miss Helen Lenoir, who is business manager and general 'right-hand man' to D'Oyly Carte, who produced *Pinafore* and *The Pirates* for Gilbert and Sullivan and also started *Billee Taylor* on the long and successful New York run. As most men who successfully manage operatic enterprises find it necessary to be at least six feet high, weigh two hundred pounds and

1. Philadelphia Times, 16 May 1881

have as much firmness and courage as a major-general, the general supposition abut Miss Lenoir is that she is an Amazon. But a reporter of *The Times*, who called on her to ask a question or two about the benefit performance which is to be tendered to the lady next week by the various companies singing *Billee Taylor,* not the Gilbert and Sullivan operas in and round New York, found a girl as slight as Sarah Bernhardt and several inches shorter and looking to be about eighteen years old. She has recently seen her twenty second birthday within a week but is unable to claim that she weighs more than a hundred pounds. Active, without being nervous, bright, with large dark eyes that never are quiet, a face so mobile that it expresses her thoughts before she has time to speak them, small, shapely hands that must find something to do even when their owner is as leisure, and Miss Lenoir is the incarnation of intelligent industry.

"Story," she laughingly echoed in response to the reporter's request for the history of her life. "I haven't any" I simply am a girl who could never endure to lounge about indoors and fold my hands – that is all."

"But," persisted the reporter, "something unusual must have placed you in a business position which many a man covets."

"Something? Well I don't know what it was. Except one. I was born at Nice in the south of France – a lovely old place and as stupid as it is lovely. I wanted to do something so, with my parents' permission, I went to London and began life for myself as a teacher of French, I passed an examination at London University and after that I had no trouble in obtaining pupils, but the work soon became very tiresome, not because of the quantity, but the unendurable sameness. Then I determined to go on the stage."

"With no training?"

"None but what I had given myself. Managers did not come in crowds to engage me, but having begun I resolved not to give up. At last I got an engagement and to go – where do you suppose?"

"Ireland? America?"

"Worse – a great deal worse. I contracted to go to India. They pay was not enormous, but I consoled myself with the thought that I would at least see a new country and many things strange and curious. But the manager changed his plans and I got a small part of the London stage. There was nothing in it but the salary. Then one day I heard that Mr Carte needed an assistant."

"And you applied for the position?"

"Yes. It sounds ridiculous for I was barely seventeen years old. Perhaps if I had been older I would have been less confident but anyhow I got the place and have held it ever since."

A woman's work

Isn't your work very exciting?"

The little woman shrugged her shoulders and burst into laughter "Really I don't know" said she. "I only know that it entirely agrees with me. I keep my health and spirits, generally keep my temper and am happier, I am sure, than ladies who have nothing to do."

"What are your general duties?"

Before answering Miss Lenoir looked suggestively at the desk, on which lay an open check book, a pile of bills, a route list, a number of letters and several pages of music. Finally she said: Well, I cast all of our pieces. I select the singers, the soloists as well as the choruses, and assign them their parts."

"Then you must be an accomplished musician."

"No but I have a quick ear and a true one. I can play at sight the accompaniment of any song that an applicant wishes to sing to show his or her ability and range and voice, and I don't think I have made many mistakes."

"But the public suppose that musical artists are very hard to manage – that they make life a burden to whoever has anything to do with them."

"Perhaps there are some such people in the profession, but somehow I find our operas can get along without them. Our people understand from the first that we mean business. If any of them merely want to sing in our operas as an excuse for worrying themselves or managers, they soon wake up."

My favourite interview with Helen at this period appeared on 28 February 1887, during the New York run of *Ruddygore*. Helen had long since gone back to London, but memories of her remained.

"A clear-headed woman of business, Mr Carte's right-hand man. A thin, nervous woman, in the prime of young womanhood, she looks like the typical American, with her vivacious, lively movements, rather than the slower English woman. Her eyes are big, brilliant and expressive; her conversational powers versatile and delightful, her mastery of subjects fairly magical and her energy indefatigable. This most agreeable, clever lady is none other than Miss Helen Lenoir, known on both sides of the Atlantic as the business manageress of the Savoy ventures. She goes in a few days across the Atlantic to look after the New York companies and the several businesses in America. I have always had unended respect for Miss Lenoir's ability. Since I've had the pleasure of a brief chat with her I add to that respect my honest admiration for her charm of manner and my sensibility to her absorbing personal magnetism. She is never masculine yet always brave and self-poised."

There was one other aspect where Helen made full use of her experiences when she first worked in Carte's office. Lectures by famous personalities were just as keenly demanded in the United States as they had been in London. The concept of piracy, both on the sea and in the theatre, was well understood in the United States. But in 1881 the next opera was *Patience*, where the humour was based on an aesthetic poet and the rapturous maidens who idolized him.

The outstanding aesthetic poet in London was Oscar Wilde. It is often claimed that D'Oyly Carte used Oscar Wilde as a 'sandwich-man' to publicize *Patience*. In fact, Wilde arrived in New York four days after the gala 100th performance of *Patience* at the Standard Theatre. He saw *Patience* at the Standard Theatre three days later.

So it was for the out-of-town venues where Wilde's image was used to explain what the aesthetic poet Bunthorne was like. Helen arranged these performances. The Keller cartoon from the *Wasp* of San Francisco shows Wilde on the occasion of his visit there in 1882.[2] Bunthorne was an amalgamation of different London aesthetes. Bunthorne's appearance on stage was graced by the quiff of white hair coming down from his forehead. This was a distinctive feature of the artist James McNeill Whistler. Born in Massachusetts, he had settled in London. He was famous for his credo Art for art's sake. He was a close friend of Richard and Helen D'Oyly Carte, as we shall see in Chapter 11.

Matthew Arnold was another celebrity for whom Helen arranged speaking engagements. He was famous for his poetry,

2. Wikipedia provided the cartoon.

which included 'Sohrab and Rustum', 'The Scholar Gipsy' *and* 'Balder Dead'. She wrote of him

> "he is the most recent lecturer for whom we made arrangements in the States. His frequently expressed views that the minority is always right and the majority always wrong and that the salvation of a nation depends on whether the saving minority is strong enough to effect it, were, I should fancy, scarcely calculated to find favour with a democratic community. I don't know whether he felt quite sure that there was a sufficient saving minority in the States to pull the republic through. Among the intellectual classes his addresses were an undoubted success."

Helen arranged for Oscar Wilde to give a lecture tour in the United States, and this helped to build up an understanding of the aesthetic movement there. In fact, Wilde's engagement for the lecture tour did not happen until the autumn of 1882. On 30 September 1882, Wilde received a cable

> "Responsible agent seeks to enquire if you will consider offer he makes by letter for fifty readings beginning November 1st. This is confidential. Answer."

The responsible agent was in fact was Colonel W. F. Morse. By 1882 Helen had established Carte's New York office at 1267 Broadway. The style of the cable was very definitely Helen's. As we shall see, she made extensive use of telegrams later to communicate with her touring companies. And the final one-word sentence Answer goes well with the quickness that people so often noticed in the way she worked. Wilde responded with equal speed on the following day October 1st:

> "Yes if offer good".

Helen sent a letter to Mr Forbes. Savoy Theatre, London, W.C. on 8 January 1885. 'Dear Mr Forbes.' I have booked the hall for Friday 20 February with an option for 27 February, at 12 guineas for the evening. It has 500 seats in the stalls and 80 at the side, plus a small balcony. The stalls could sell at 10/6 and make a reasonable profit. Whistler has not sent a draft of the advert yet. Mr. F. said Whistler suggested that if Mr. Carte and he managed to arrange the affair Mr. Carte should take 10% of the profit and Whistler accept the risk. This was a similar arrangement to that in

Mr. F.'s tours five years previously. However Mr. Carte only undertakes affairs where he also undertakes the risk. This was why in Mr. F.'s American tour they did not charge him any commission but let him use their office and pay Morse for any work he did for him. With the tours of Matthew Arnold, Oscar Wilde, and Sergeant Ballantine,[3] Carte accepted the risk and profits were equally shared with the lecturer. Mr. Carte would arrange a tour for Whistler in America or anywhere else on this basis. She admired the lecture greatly. Mr. F. may show this letter to Whistler and remind him to send his draft of advert and tickets.

3. Ballantine acted as Counsel for Sir Charles Mordaunt in the notorious divorce case against Lady Mordaunt. She informed him that he was not the father of her child. She admitted that she had committed adultery with a number of men, including the Prince of Wales, 'often, and in open day.'

11

Helen's value to Richard D'Oyly Carte

Carte's appreciation of Helen as a manager is illustrated by letters exchanged in 1886.[1] Leslie Baily wrote: "Letters that now passed between Carte and Helen Lenoir threw a charming and amusing light on their relationship".

Carte's first letter to Helen pointed out that he could not have done the business at all, or at any on the same scale, without her help and he now (1886) suggested a new arrangement by which he would pay Miss Lenoir £1,000 a year, plus 10 per cent commission on business in all the theatres. It was a princely income for a working woman in Victorian times, and Miss Lenoir replied that it was too much.

> Carte to Miss Lenoir:
> "Knowing your particular disposition as I do, I can quite understand your hesitation in receiving this amount. Probably most outsiders would think your line of conduct absolutely quixotic, but I fully appreciate your motives. You object to receive more than you think you have fairly earned. I am quite willing to fall in with your views in this respect. I do not desire that you should be under obligation to me."

He then suggested that the proposal should be referred to arbitration by a business acquaintance of them both. Unfortunately there is no record of the outcome of this remarkable proposal. It must have been satisfactory to Carte and Helen.

---

1. *The Gilbert and Sullivan Book* Leslie Baily. Cassell & Co 1952. Page 163

In today's money, according to the online Bank of England inflation calculator, the salary of £1,000 per year to Helen was the equivalent of £172,921. No wonder Helen thought it was too much.

Helen's experience in managing several different companies simultaneously touring several different North American towns stood her in good stead when she took on similar arrangements in Great Britain and Ireland. It was perhaps more difficult to carry out the arrangements in North America because the distances were so much greater. On the other hand, the British branch lines, owned by a variety of companies, often did not connect smoothly.

Helen's influence on the British touring companies began much earlier than has been recognised previously, as the following paragraph shows. B Company's visit to Wigan took place in the three weeks from 26 December 1882.

The following extract from a regular feature in *The Stage* places Helen's arrival on to the British touring scene as late in 1882[2]:

"A correspondent reminds me that it was shortly after the accession of the late Mrs Carte to directorial influence that the 'seven shows for six' came into being. I do remember it well. What a misunderstanding there was at Wigan one New Year's week, when the Christmas Day was stopped as a sixth and the extra matinee was paid for at half a seventh, i.e. one fourteenth! But the matter was soon put right, and everybody was paid in full for Christmas Day when the head office interfered."

This anecdote refers to B Company's visit to Wigan which started on 26 December 1882. It places the start of Helen Lenoir's directorial influence as shortly before Christmas 1882.

Helen's eye for detail came in with the foundation of E Company, which started with performances of *Patience* and *Iolanthe* on 1 January 1885. Whereas the other companies would spend up to three weeks in one venue, E Company could do three venues in a week! For example in the week beginning 19 January 1885, they did venues in Wales – 4 days in Newport, 1 in Neath and 1 in Llanelli. They played the first provincial production of *The Mikado* on 22 May at Northampton. One notable performer was Lucy Carr Shaw (sister of George Bernard Shaw) as Ella in *Patience* and Celia in *Iolanthe*.

2. *The Stage*, The Music Box by James M Glover. London 15 May 1913, page 23

In 1885 E Company moved the venues 95 times. They contributed to the profitability of D'Oyly Carte because they reached audiences who did not live close to the main towns. It made people feel they were they were part of the G&S public.

Helen had a soft spot for the actors in E Company. And, as we shall see in subsequent chapters, they loved her.

On 21 August 1885, precisely two days after Richard D'Oyly Carte had attended the New York premier production of *The Mikado*, his wife Blanche Julia Carte (née Prowse) died of pneumonia. She had been in poor health for several years.[3] She was only 32 years old. She died at a stately country home named St Albans Bank on the banks of the Thames near Teddington. The house was not a nursing home. It was owned by Thomas Allen and his son (also Thomas Allen) from about 1807 to 1899. They occupied the house sometimes and rented it. Carte may have expected his wife's health to be well monitored while he was away in America.

Blanche Carte was the daughter of William Prowse (1801–1886), music publisher and musical instrument maker. Prowse had entered into partnership with Robert William Keith to found the Keith Prowse Company. It is likely that this firm sold tickets for *The Mikado* and other Gilbert and Sullivan operas.

A poster survives from 1 February 1866 showing that Carte had appeared in an amateur performance of a farce by Thomas John Williams entitled *Ici on parle français*. John Lawrence Toole played the principal part as Joe Spriggins. Blanche Prowse played Anna Maria, the servant. She was aged only 13. Carte married her in 1871. They had two sons Lucas (born 1872) and Rupert (born 1876).[4]

3. Paper presented by Colin Prestige at International Conference, Kansas University, May 1950, 'D'Oyly Carte and the Pirates', published by University of Kansas Libraries page 135
4. Gilbert & Sullivan, A dual biography. Michael Ainger, Oxford University Press, New York 2002, page 75

In the summer of 1881 Blanche took the two boys for a seaside holiday at Broadstairs.[5] This town of Kent was a fashionable resort, much visited by Londoners in the Victorian period. Blanche has not, as far as I can discover, featured in any other reports. I wondered whether she had suffered post natal depression, but the Broadstairs holiday shows that Carte trusted her to care for the boys.

After the death of Blanche, Carte and Helen continued to work together, with no obvious change in their relationship. They shared the same determination to see the operas and the D'Oyly Carte Company succeed.

The letters from 1886, quoted at the beginning of this chapter, show that Carte had the very highest regard for Helen's business ability. He had made a very generous offer, but it was on strictly commercial basis. When he wrote in his second letter that he did not want Helen to be under obligation to him, it was the first sign that personal considerations were coming into play.

5. Ainger, pages 201 and 251

12

Helen & Richard D'Oyly Carte: marriage, honeymoon & family

In 1990 I visited the Pierpont Morgan Library in New York. The librarian Rick Wilson (Frederic Woodbridge Wilson) produced two leather bound volumes. These were Lucas D'Oyly Carte's diary for 1888 from which I copied these extracts in 1990. They focus on Lucas's life at home with his father and Helen Lenoir, and especially any references to the Savoy and London theatre life. The photograph was taken on the Carte family's yacht in Portsmouth Harbour in 1891. It is thus within three years from when he wrote his 1888 diary.

I have omitted some entries about school life at Winchester where Lucas was a boarder. Lucas was just 16 at the start of the year; his brother Rupert (in the diary he is referred to as Frater, Toups, Toopie and Rutie). I have added a few notes, based on information given to me by Peter Parker, whose father Stanley Parker became Secretary and Treasurer of the D'Oyly Carte Company after being recruited to the Savoy organisation by Helen c 1907 The diary is of particular interest because 1888 is the year when Richard D'Oyly Carte married Helen. They show how Helen had become part of the D'Oyly Carte family life even in the first months of the year. They also give a picture of how she fitted smoothly into their family life. For example, there are four dates when Lucas received a letter from Helen while he was at Winchester College. There are none from his father because Helen was capable of keeping the family in touch with one another.

> Sunday 1 Jan: Breakfast 11.30. Walked 6 or 7 miles. On our walk went and saw Christie, Sir Arthur (s 10/-) and Gilbert.

s 10/- = sub of ten shillings. This seems to have been Sullivan's usual gift to Lucas.

> 2 Jan: Bought some armchairs etc. HL saw about chintzes, and about carpenter Sheldon.
> 5 Jan: Supper at 8 with Auntie Bd (?) and HL.

There are several references in the diary to Auntie Bd and Auntie Ba. She/They do (es) not show in Richard D'Oyly Carte's side of the family. Peter has suggested they may be one or two sisters of Lucas's mother, Blanche (née Prowse) who died in August 1885. Bd and Ba might be the same aunt: Brenda is a possibility.

> 7 Jan: Whistler came to breakfast. Looked over chintzes et tablecloths etc. Dinner with list including HL.

James McNeill Whistler did the interior design for Carte's house at 4 Adelphi Terrace. He was a good friend of Richard D'Oyly Carte and Helen.

> 8 Jan: Walked from Weybridge, where we inspected the island, to Sunbury (per Towpath) where we had lunch at Magpie, whence to Hampton Court (Tagg's Island) where we had drinks, and then took train to Waterloo. Billiards.

Carte bought the island in the Thames at Weybridge, and used it as a country house.

> 9 Jan: We went with Father and HL to *Arabian Nights* at Comedy. (M)

M = moderate?

> 10 Jan Went to Lock's (Rupert's <u>first</u> tallhat). Mr and Mrs Gunn arrived from Ireland.
> 11 Jan Tea with Mrs Gunn and Miss Hoffmeister.

Mrs Gunn as Bessie Sudlow had sung the Plaintiff in one of Carte's earliest tours of *Trial by Jury* in Dublin, where she met and married Michael Gunn.

13 Jan Went to Surrey pantomime *Sindbad the Sailor* with Gunns etc. Dinner at Simpsons.

16 Jan Went to Empire in evening with Mr and Mrs Gunn.

17 Jan Went to Covent Garden panto *Jack and the Beanstalk* (VM) with Gunn's.

18 Jan Gilbert's party: enormous fun. Saw lots of people I know. Bed 1.0. V.V.V.V.V.G.

22 Jan Mr and Mrs Gunn had dinner with us at 6 – and then went back to Ireland.

23 Jan I and Frater succeeded in eating five helps of cold beef each.

24 Jan Still having our meals in the 'Study' on account of dining room being painted.

Whistler's design was being put into effect.

25 Jan Father and I went to Turkish Baths (Savoy) and dined afterwards with HL at Café Royal.
LUCAS THEN WENT BACK TO WINCHESTER

2 Feb Had intended playing Association at John's with L. Gowers etc: but put off on account of hard frost. I played bat fives.

5 Feb Wrote to HL and Father.

9 Feb Received letters from Malan, and HL.

14 Feb *Mrs Jaramie's Genie* – the new farce was produced with great success, as HL tells me in her letter of 18th. Met young Ricketts etc.

19 Feb Female fainted in Cathedral and had to be carried out – she was a good 20 minutes coming to.

23 Feb I received the expected telegram to go to London tomorrow, and late leave, also on spec of Dentist. In evening I received 20/- for going to London tomorrow.

24 Feb Went up to London by 7.23 (Very cold) train. On my arrival at home I found Guv in bed, whom I roused up. At 11.15 went to Dentist (Mr Morton Smale).

17 Mar *The Pirates of Penzance* came out at the Savoy with great success.

This was the First Revival of *The Pirates of Penzance*, and the first time it had ever been played at the Savoy Theatre.

25 Mar Wrote letters as usual to Father, Frater, Auntie Bd and Miss Lenoir before 11 o'clock Cathedral.

28 Mar Ate 6 sausages at 8.45. Finally I sociused Patty, Ian and Masher up in a fly to catch the 9.16 train. Arrived home at 11.45 where I found Toopie already arrived. Went to Father at the Theatre and then on to Miles (Tailors) in Brooke Street where I met Kug and Nater and Ian, and having ordered some clothes we returned to lunch. Billie came to Dinner and Genie and Pirates with us afternoon and evening.

No, I don't know the word sociused. It may have been Winchester slang, meaning he went together with these school friends to the station at the end of term. Brooke Street is the way Lucas wrote Brook Street.

29 Mar Bought some daffodils at the florist's under Dr Hall's place, and gave them to Miss Lenoir. Went to Dentist (Morton Smale) at 12.0. Mr Fladgate and HL and Father came to a midday hot dinner.

Peter Parker remembers that there was a Fladgate & Co in his father's day. He believes they were Carte's solicitors, or possibly his stockbroker. This meeting may have been in preparation for the marriage of Father and HL. Significant perhaps that this lunch is listed as one of the four events up to end March in Lucas's Analysis at the end of the diary.

30 Mar Had dinner at Gattis with HL, Uncle Henry and Father and Trapp. Afterwards played cards with Mockett: After which we relapsed into a frenzied fit of method-less madness and hilarity. Bed about 11.15. Made a break of 11 at Billiards and two of 8.

Uncle Henry = Henry Williams Carte, b 12/01/1856, d 03/03/1926. Fifth child of the marriage of Richard Carte (b 1808, Silchester, d 1891 at Reigate) and Eliza née Jones (b 1814, Gower Street, London, d 24/01/1885 at Hastings. Richard D'Oyly Carte was their first child, so Uncle Henry is a genuine uncle. Peter Parker thinks Mockett was butler/major domo for Richard D'Oyly Carte.

31 Mar Took the midday train to Sandwich.

1 Apr We rose with a rather late lark at about 6.30.

2 Apr Caught 8.55 train from Canterbury to London.

3 Apr Went in the evening to the Avenue, and saw Arthur Roberts in *The Old Guard*. Bed 12. α

α is the alpha sign that Lucas uses as a variation for V.V.V.V.V.G. He later uses ß (beta) for V. Fairly Good, Γ (gamma = English C) and Σ (epsilon) which equates to V.N.B.G.

5 Apr In the afternoon had a riding lesson. Went to the Dentist in Seymour Street quite close where he stopped my third tooth with gold. Went in the evening with Auntie Lizzie and Toopie to the Vaudeville where we saw *Joseph's Sweetheart*. It was very fairly good. Tom Thorne as the clergyman was VG. Bed 12.15. α-

Aunt Lizzie was Eliza Carte, sixth child of Richard and Eliza Carte, Lucas's genuine aunt. *Joseph's Sweetheart* opened on 8th March. It was written by Robert Buchanan and played at the Vaudeville Theatre. Tom Thorne was eldest brother of Carte's Number 1 touring comedian George Thorne (George turns up on 7 Apr).

6 Apr Breakfast 9.30. Father had breakfast in bed. At 1.15 we went to the Savoy and went on to catch the 2 something train from Euston to Manchester. On the way, while we were driving in one of Wolfe's carriages, the horse fell, and we were some considerable time getting him on to his feet again. We had a special carriage reserved for us by Mr Rich, the manager at Euston. Arrived in Manchester in four hours' time (i.e. soon after 6). This train is a <u>very</u> good one indeed. We had some nice rooms at the Grand and a nice dinner all ready for us. We went to see *Patience* played at the Prince's in evening: Mrs Fitz-Patrick was Patience.

7 Apr Went out with Father down Market Place to discover the swimming baths. After walking for over a mile, we came upon a dingy, twopenny first class fourpence on Friday's place, which did not entice us enough to go in. We have come to the conclusion that we have never seen a filthier, gloomier place than Manchester.

At 2 we went to see Miss Maitland (the usual actress in the company) as Patience. At 5.30 we had a nice dinner. At 7.30 we went to see Miss Queensbeam as Patience. Afterwards George Thorne came around to the hotel to see us.

It was the Number 1 touring company (C Company) that Carte went to see in Manchester. This tour ran from 27th February to 16th June. Rhoda Maitland was the principal soprano playing Patience in this tour. At first glance, it seems puzzling that she should be pushed into the Saturday matinee for Carte to check/audition two unknowns on the two most important evenings of the week in a very important venue. George Low has suggested what I believe is the correct explanation. Rollins and Witts have a M. Fitzpatrick singing Rose Maybud in the C Company tour briefly in March 1887. She is quickly superseded by Margaret Cockburn who sang Rose Maybud from some time in March 1887 until November. George believes that M. Fitzpatrick is the married name of Margaret Cockburn. She went on a continental tour in November 1887, returning to England in February 1888. There was no obvious vacancy for her in the Carte touring companies. Evelyn Kingsbury had taken over Rose Maybud from her in November 1887. So the first Patience that Lucas heard is Margaret Cockburn – it is quite likely that she was introduced to him by her married name. The Saturday night Patience is Evelyn Kingsbury – Queensbeam sounds a very unlikely name, and Lucas may have altered it either for schoolboy humour or because he did not remember it properly. So Carte went to Manchester to resolve what he wanted to do about the three Patiences who had sung with C Company within the previous five months. In the C Company tour starting 30th July 1888, Margaret Cockburn went out as lead soprano, singing Mabel, Yum-Yum and Patience. Rhoda Maitland took secondary soprano roles: Isabel, Peep-Bo and Lady Ella. Evelyn Kingsbury (or Queensbeam) made no further Carte appearances. Sorry this is a rather lengthy note, but it does demonstrate the degree to which Carte was involved in the management of the No 1 touring company, even in 1888.

8 Apr Came up to town by the 12.15 train (Pullman) arriving St Pancras 5 o'clock.

9 Apr Went to the Dentist's and had my fourth tooth stopped with Gold. Went to Turkish Bath (Savoy).

10 Apr Went to see the doctor (Dr Barrett of 3 Tavistock Square) about my chest. After lunch went to Dentist leaving Rupert at Savoy to go on to Truman's about his tooth. At 3.30 arrived at Morton Smale's and had my fifth tooth stopped. Walked back from Seymour Street to Savoy. And dinner out at Smith's in a private Room in the Strand. HL and Father were there.

11 Apr Dinner with HL, Father, us, Mr Stanley, and Mr Fladgate. Afterwards Father of his <u>intentions</u> for the following day. Billiards.

The next day's entry is written in red ink.

12 Apr Breakfast about 9: Went to Dr Barrett's about my chest and was back by 11.
   At 11.30 <u>Father</u> was married to <u>Miss Lenoir</u> (Miss Couper-Black) by Rev Henry White in the Chapel Royal, Savoy. Sir <u>Arthur Sullivan</u> and Sir <u>James Caird</u> and <u>Lady Caird</u> were present only. Immediately afterwards they returned to Adelphi Terrace and had <u>lunch</u> – <u>the servants knew nothing about it</u>: we all started off (Sir <u>Arthur</u> having given me 10/-) in the <u>Midday train</u> to Dover, where we strolled about and had dinner and went to bed at about 11.

End of entry written in red.

Underlining and double underlining is as written by Lucas. Incidentally, in the early 1980s, I asked Albert Truelove (Dame Bridget's Private Secretary) to find out if she knew how her father felt about Helen. Dame Bridget said the two boys adored her. Sir James and Lady Caird were friends of the Couper Black family in Wigtown. The Caird family owned one of the Scottish engineering companies. One member of the family, John Caird, had been Principal of Glasgow University since 1873. His brother Edward, became Master of Balliol College Oxford in 1893.

13 Apr Breakfast at 9.30: Helen went up to London by 12 something train. In the morning we engaged a Deck Cabin on board the "Invicta". Received telegram from Trapp to say O.K. Excellent passage across to Calais. (Toups hardly ill). I strolled about deck the whole time. Arriving at Calais we had a good meal at the Station Buffet, which is excellent: thence in a coupé to the Gare du Nord, Paris: drove straight to the hotel de Lille et d'Albion; where we engaged some very good rooms. In the evening we strolled along the Rue St Honoré as far as Voisin's, where we had a splendid dinner (best oysters ever known). Bed 11 a
14 Apr Dejeuner in a restaurant in the Palais Royal. Took a fiacre and drove to the Bois de Boulogne. On our way back

we counted 10 Weddings and noticed the Bridegrooms all in Evening dress. Dined at the Maison Marquerry VG and saw *Les Puits qui Parle* at the Nouveautés, after a cup of coffee at an open air café. Bed: 12. α +

French accents and grammar are as in Lucas's diary.

15 Apr At about 10 o'clock we drove to the Morgue, where we saw two bodies: then walked across to Notre Dame which was like an Icehouse inside, so cold, so much so that we had to dash round the Place outside to warm ourselves before ascending the tower (4d each). On reaching the top we had a splendid view. We also saw the big bell from Sebastopol. At about 12.30 we déjeuned at a small Duval (VG). Then wandered about among old quays and curiosity shops on the further bank of the Seine. Returned to Hotel. Guv wrote letters, and we bought maps etc. Went to Station and met Helen (with a huge bunch of violets). Had a 3 franc dinner at Rochers (VG) and went to the Nouveau Cirque (water: VG). Bed 12. α+

Mon 16 Apr Café au lait at 9.0. Got up and dressed and had déjeuner in the hotel at about 12. After which we took a steamer (3 halfpence) from the Louvre to Auteuil. On our way we saw the new tower of Eifel in progress of building, and also the various other buildings for the Exhibition of 1889. Guv with Frater went to see about seats for the Opera and afterwards wrote letters. Helen, myself, and Frater then went and purchased various presents in the Palais Royal and in the Rue de Rivoli. Dined at Bignon's (VG), and afterwards went to Opera House where we saw *L'Africaine* (VG): De Reské was the tenor; he has one of the finest voices I have ever heard. Bed: 1.0. α+

17 Apr Café au lait at 8.30 with Eggs. Went off with Mockett in 9.40 train. Arrived at Amiens – 20 minutes for déjeuner for which we had "Poulet" and "Haricots Verts". Saw some man from school on platform. Frater was <u>very</u> cut up about leaving the Guv and Helen, and was unable to eat anything on that account. Arrived at Boulogne and found a cabin engaged for us on the boat. Frater was sick, I believe, simply because he remained all the time in the cabin. Had some light refreshment at Folkestone, and travelled in an <u>excellent</u> 2nd class carriage to London.

> Had dinner at Upton's in Strand, packed everything at Adelphi Terrace, calling on Gunn's, got to D.P.R at 10. Bed 10.30. a-

D.P.R = home of Richard Carte at 2 Dartmouth Park Road (now NW5).

> 18 Apr Geoffrey was very pleased with the shoes we brought him. Aunt Blanche and her child Olive were staying there. On our way to the Savoy we found Mrs Gunn at home but Haidee was very shy and blankly refused to come and see us. Picked up Parkins at Savoy and caught 5.50 to Winchester.

Geoffrey is the son of Henry Williams Carte, b 1885 and living at 2 Dartmouth Park Road. Aunt Blanche (b 06/03/1846, d 28/07/1925) is the second child of Richard and Eliza Carte, another of Lucas's genuine aunts. She married the Rev Thomas Pateshall Monnington (a 2nd cousin), and it was the Rev Monnington who carried out the funeral service for Eliza Carte at Fairlight near Hastings in 1885.

> 23 Aug Rained all the morning. Father went up by 10.11. Bertie Sullivan came down in evening. Played tennis with Mockett and Henry (two sets) in afternoon.

Bertie Sullivan is Sullivan's nephew Herbert.

> 28 Aug Went up the Wey (canalised) in Canoe with Rupert and Bertie S. above the second Lock (by the M.U.) where we shot a small weir and explored the big lake there.
> 30 Aug Had an imitation home-made Turkish bath in the spare bedroom. Played Tennis afterwards with Rupert and Mockett and Henry. Father has not missed coming down to Dinner here yet.
> 31 Aug Bertie Sullivan's Birthday (He is 20): At least so he says. Went by boat, towing, to Barrington's Tennis party at Laleham: Mr Faithful, Hunt, Robertson (and his leggy dog) and Mr and Mrs B themselves. Played several sets. Beat Rupert in a single 6 – 1. Lovely fine day.

Arthur Jacobs gives Herbert Sullivan's year of birth as 1866, so Lucas's doubts about Bertie's age seem to have been justified!

Rutland Barrington's mother's maiden name was Faithfull, so the tennis-playing Mr Faithful may have been an uncle or cousin of Barrington.

> 1 Sep Had a fearful smash-up coming downhill from station on tricycle. Waited round about in expectation of Father's early return from town, which did not come off.
> 2 Sep Rained hard all day. Went down in 'Merlin' to Chappell and had tea: whence by Train home.
> Monday 3 Sep Went up to town with Father and Rupert. Bertie stopped down. Helen came back from Devonshire, where she had been staying since Friday. Took Airgun to Shop to be repaired. Heard reading of new piece. Came down after lunch at Simpson's. Went out in launch with Bertie to Chertsey, and back.

Helen's family had lived near Taunton before they went to Australia. Her aunt Matilda Black died at Clifton near Bristol on 18.12.1887, but Helen would still have had friends in the West Country in 1888. The New Piece premiered at the Savoy on 3rd October. Its title? – *The Yeomen of the Guard*.[1]

> 19 Sep Came up to Town in Midday. Went back to School + 30/-

There is a pasted in list of Rev J.T. Bramston's house at Winchester that includes:

> D'Oyly Carte
> Leveson-Gower sen, sec, tert, jun
> Bonham-Carter sen, jun
> Weatherby sen, jun
> Wigram sen, sec, jun

Bonham-Carter may have belonged to the family that included Lothian Bonham-Carter who played for Hampshire and England. In modern times Helena Bonham-Carter is a successful film actress. She played Bellatrix Lestrange in the *Harry Potter* film series, and won a BAFTA award for her portrayal of Queen Elizabeth in *The King's Speech*.

---

1. Illustration from The Savoy Operas. Percy Fitzgerald, Chatto & Windus London 1894, page 191

THE YEOMEN OF THE SAVOY

3 Dec there have been 3 big events this ½
1. Big Booze Row (after XV)
2. We won all Matches
3. Applause Row
5 Dec Father and Helen came down in the evening – went to dinner with him and her.
Thurs 6 Dec Went up to Breakfast at 'George' with Guv, and Helen, and Trapp. Chapel at 10. Afterwards went and

looked at our VI v College. We won 14 – 10: Podge made the most extraordinary kick ever seen. Guv and Helen arrived Lunch. Had Dinner with them in evening. They went up to Town. Showed Helen over our house. This is the first time she has been down.

18 Dec Results at 4 o'clock. I was 4th in Du Boulay's and got my remove. Kuggel and Fred Gower were 9th and 10th respectively. Podge was junior. House supper in Evening in honour of Tim and Bate who are leaving.

19 Dec Got to sleep at 4.30. Got up at 8.45: only just time to hurry and dress, and get breakfast on off to the 9.16 train, with Fred Gower and Polly etc. Kugs too late to get up for this train. Went straight home and found the second Breakfast nearly ready. The new dog 'Gup' agrees with Trapp – is a bitch – is ragged-looking – is bad-mannered – is to be sent away tomorrow. Met Fred at Aquarium. Went to Theatre to see *Yeomen* with Bruiser and Fred. VG-. Fred slept in Rutie's Bed. Bed 12.15

20 Dec Fred Gower went away in morning. 2 Kuggas, Potty and G. Bonham came and played billiards etc, and tea. Rutie came home just after two Kugs had left. Went to Savoy (Box A) to *Yeomen* in evening. Bed 1.0

21 Dec Put Room Straight. Bought Items etc.

22 Dec Ordinary 2 breakfasts. Yesterday Rupert went to Savoy to meet a Master of his from School. For whom he got a seat.

23 Dec 1st breakfast about 10. Second about 11.30. Walked about in the Park (Regent's) while Father and Helen went in and saw Mrs Fladgate and Lu etc etc. Billiards. Dinner. Billiards. Bed 11.45

24 Dec Slept till 9. Only had one breakfast and that at 10. Billie came at 11.30. Guv and Helen awfully busy at Theatre, and so altogether we did not buy presents as intended, but Christmas cards at stores. Lunch at 1.30. Afterwards Billie went away and we sent Xmas cards etc. Issued invitations to Servants for Xmas Eve party, but did not come off.

Uncle Robert came in Evening, and we had dinner at 7.45 – 8. Father came down late to dinner and menu was:
Consommé
Faisant à la Getana
Truffles
Bed after billiards at 11.15. Made up accounts.

Uncle Robert was perhaps a brother of Lucas's mother

Tuesday 25 Dec Xmas Day. 1st Breakfast at 9. Walked a mile in 15 minutes up and down Adelphi Terrace. Sent family and servants Xmas cards. 2nd Breakfast at 12 about. Billiards. Father, Helen and Uncle Robert went out for a walk, to Sir Arthur's by the way. We played Billiards till 1.30, went out into St James's Park. Came back by Strand, and dinner at 7.30. Uncle Robert here.

26 Dec As usual, 2 Breakfasts. Bertie S came and played billiards in the afternoon. In Evening we had the Servants Card Party, with Mockett, Mrs Creed and Henry in our room. Bed 11.45. Kept awake till my birthday hour struck.

27 Dec My Birthday. I am 17. Finished putting up Soldiers. Bought Sand. Mrs Creed made me an elegant Birthday. Cake. In evening went to the 'Den' at Toole's with Rupert and Uncle Robert. Jack Gunn was acting: V.G. Acting. Bed 1.0

28 Dec Got up at 9.30. 1st breakfast (porridge) at 9.45. 2nd Breakfast at 12.30. Guv and Helen at B.H. Billie came at 12.30 and had breakfast with us. Afterwards we bought presents in Bedford Street (Civil Service Supply Stores: £4 only). Back at 3.30. Found Jack Gunn and Rutie playing billiards. Tea at 4. Billie went. I went with her as far as Lowther Arcade. Came back to dinner after seeing Jack Gunn to end of Strand. Dinner 7.30. Went to Savoy and saw *Yeomen* for 3rd time. Met Bonham-C there. Bed 12.30. Bertie S came to dinner and theatre afterwards.

Sat 29 Dec Got up at ¼ to ten. Breakfast (only one) at 10 o'clock. Ticketed presents to send away to children. Went out and bought Mockett a Star Razor. Uncle Robert went off to Brighton. Lunch at 1.15. Bertie Sullivan came in the afternoon: played skittles in the hall: and billiards. B.S. stopped till 6. We had dinner at 6.15 – 30. Went to first night of *Macbeth* at Lyceum. Sir Arthur's Incidental Music and Irving and Ellen Terry as Macbeth and Lady Macbeth. Walked home. Father and Helen had gone there in Stall. We (I and Rutie) sat in the same box with Mr Smythe and Bertie. Got a letter from Bertie Lambert yesterday, who is in Montrose (Scotland) on account of his growth on Throat. Billiards: Sandwiches: Bed 12.45

Walter Smythe was Sullivan's secretary.

> 30 Dec Woke at 9 and got up at 9. Rupert would not get up:
> wrote diary. Rutie came down about ¼ to 11, and we
> walked 1320 yards up and down the terrace. Only one
> breakfast and that at 11.15. Went for a long walk – partly
> hansom – as far as 'Welsh Harp' where we lunched
> heavily on Hot Roast Beef at 2.30. Walked part of way
> back, and as it was getting dark we bussed it from
> Kilburn.

The Welsh Harp is about 5 miles (straight line) from Dartmouth
Park Road. Lucas would have had to take a longer journey even in
the 1880s, and also climb some hilly areas around Hampstead
Heath.

> 31 Dec Very foggy in morning. Did not go out at all. Help
> Rupert put up his soldiers. Rup went out disguised as
> burglar with a bulls-eye lantern. Did not go to the Theatre
> in Evening. Fog at its worst. Hancock came to billiards.
> Dinner. Bed 11.45.
> The Worst Fog Ever Seen.
> Jack Gunn came in the afternoon.
> Pages of Year's Analysis
> Jan 11 D Jones's Party: No Dancing.
> Feb 14 Pancakes. *Mrs Jaramie's Genie* at Savoy produced.
> Mar 28 Pirates and Genie in evening
> Mar 29 Fladgate to Lunch: & HL & Guv.

Lucas was back in London by 19th August, and played tennis with
Bertie Sullivan on 23rd August and went on a boat trip with him
on 28th August, but he did not record any thought about his
mother just three years after she died.

There is no mention of the building of the Savoy Hotel, which
was in full swing by the end of 1888 (it opened in August 1889).
The site of the new hotel was very close to the Carte's home at 4
Adelphi Terrace (now replaced by the Shell-Mex building).

An unusual memento of Richard and Helen's wedding has
recently come to light.

This is the text of an Address presented to Mr & Mrs D'Oyly
Carte with a Pair of Candlesticks

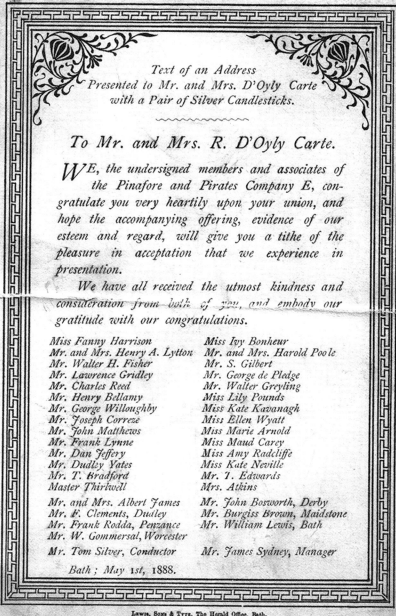

Text of an Address
Presented to Mr. and Mrs. D'Oyly Carte
with a Pair of Silver Candlesticks.

To Mr. and Mrs. R. D'Oyly Carte.

*W*E, *the undersigned members and associates of the Pinafore and Pirates Company E, congratulate you very heartily upon your union, and hope the accompanying offering, evidence of our esteem and regard, will give you a tithe of the pleasure in acceptation that we experience in presentation.*

We have all received the utmost kindness and consideration from both of you, and embody our gratitude with our congratulations.

Miss Fanny Harrison	*Miss Ivy Bonheur*
Mr. and Mrs. Henry A. Lytton	*Mr. and Mrs. Harold Poole*
Mr. Walter H. Fisher	*Mr. S. Gilbert*
Mr. Lawrence Gridley	*Mr. George de Pledge*
Mr. Charles Reed	*Mr. Walter Greyling*
Mr. Henry Bellamy	*Miss Lily Pounds*
Mr. George Willoughby	*Miss Kate Kavanagh*
Mr. Joseph Correze	*Miss Ellen Wyatt*
Mr. John Matthews	*Miss Marie Arnold*
Mr. Frank Lynne	*Miss Maud Carey*
Mr. Dan Jeffery	*Miss Amy Radcliffe*
Mr. Dudley Yates	*Miss Kate Neville*
Mr. T. Bradford	*Mr. T. Edwards*
Master Thirlwell	*Mrs. Atkins*
Mr. and Mrs. Albert James	*Mr. John Bosworth, Derby*
Mr. F. Clements, Dudley	*Mr. Burgiss Brown, Maidstone*
Mr. Frank Rodda, Penzance	*Mr. William Lewis, Bath*
Mr. W. Gommersal, Worcester	
Mr. Tom Silver, Conductor	*Mr. James Sydney, Manager*

Bath ; May 1st, 1888.

Lewis, Sons & Tyte, The Herald Office, Bath.

To Mr and Mrs R D'Oyly Carte

We, the undersigned members of the Pinafore and Pirate Company E Congratulate you very heartily on your union and hope the accompanying offering, evidence of our esteem and regard, will give you a taste of the pleasure in anticipation that we experience in anticipation.

We have all received the utmost kindness and consideration from both of you, and embody our gratitude with our congratulations.

The address is dated Bath, May 1st 1888

In total there are 37 names on the list, three of which are married couples. Henry Lytton is of course married to Louie Henri. Albert James and Harold Poole are long-standing members of D'Oyly Carte companies, but there is no record of their wives' names: They may have been choristers.

It is fascinating that six of the names are listed with a town beside them. The towns are Dudley, Penzance, Worcester, Derby, Maidstone and Bath. The company is E Company and they had visited Dudley on 3 and 4 February: they spent three days in Worcester on April 19, 20 and 21. George Low suggests that these may have been recruited as potential managers for the touring companies.

There may of course be other mementos from other companies which have not yet come to light. It seems particularly appropriate that it is E company's tribute that has surfaced in the 21st century bearing we shall see in Chapter 15 that Helen had a special affection for E Company, and they for her.

13

Helen & Richard as entrepreneurs & safety officers

Helen and Richard had set out to build a new theatre. But in fact they created a whole new environment as this remarkable picture shows. It appeared in *The Illustrated London News* on 24 April 1865.

It shows work in progress on the intercept sewer and Thames Embankment which was completed in July 1871. The work was carried out by the legendary London engineer Sir Joseph Bazalgette. The Embankment Gardens were opened in 1874. On that date Richard D'Oyly Carte had established his concert agency in Charing Cross. Helen was living in North Bristol. She did not start her studies at London University until the following year.

The picture was on page 369, and on page 370 there is almost a full column of text giving details of the construction of the Northern Intercept Sewer. The article explains that the laying of the first stone in front of Whitehall Stairs had taken place on 30 July 1864. By 1865 an outer wall, formed of caissons and intermediate timber piles, had been built and was used for steam engines which were used to carry bricks and stone from barges. There was plenty of space for the sewer, gas and water pipes and electricity cables. Throughout the construction, care was being taken to achieve standards of safety and solidity that exceeded the minimum. The low level sewer had a fall of 1 in 2610, 2 feet per mile. If Helen had seen the report, she would have been truly impressed.

The site had had a chequered history. King Henry III had granted the land to Peter, Count of Savoy, in 1246. The palace built there later became the home of Prince Edmund, In the 14th century, when the Strand was paved as far as the Savoy, it was the residence of John of Gaunt, Richard II's uncle and the nation's power broker. The Savoy was the most magnificent mansion in England, famous for its tapestries, jewels and ornaments. Geoffrey Chaucer began writing *The Canterbury Tales* while working at the Savoy Palace as a clerk. However, all of its structure except the chapel was destroyed by the Peasants' Revolt of 1381, when Wat Tyler led an army of over 50 thousand men protesting against high taxation.

John of Gaunt was the father of four illegitimate children. They all took Beaufort as their family name. It was at 11 Beaufort Street that Carte had his office, and at one stage Carte intended to use the Beaufort name for the new theatre that he planned to build on the newly cleared site.

In about 1505, Henry VII had a hospital built in the palace ruins, and part of the old palace was used for a military prison in the 18th century. Daniel Defoe wrote in *A Tour through London about the year 1725* "The Savoy may be said to be, not a House, but a little Town, being parted into innumerable Tenements and Apartments". In 1864 a fire burned everything except the stone walls, and the site sat empty until Carte bought the freehold of the site, then known as 'Beaufort Buildings'.

Carte's primary purpose in buying the site was that he wanted to build a theatre which would be suitable and safe for presenting Gilbert and Sullivan operas in the future. In 1877 Carte looked over a site within the precincts of the ancient Royal Palace of the Savoy. He arranged for the architect Walter Emden to carry out the planning and building of a theatre. Emden lacked experience as a theatre architect. His only theatre buildings were the Globe Theatre in Newcastle Street (1870) in the rickety maze of buildings that were replaced in 1902 by the development of the Aldwych, and the Civic Theatre in Barnsley (1877). True, Emden was later to establish himself as a successful London theatre architect with the Garrick Theatre in 1889 for W. S. Gilbert and the Duke of York's Theatre in 1892.[1]

Emden was not only short of experience, he was also short of cash. In April 1878 he was adjudicated bankrupt but nonetheless he continued with Carte's theatre. He obtained an assurance from the Board of Works that they would open a new street on the south side, provided that Carte came up with half the cost. Carte sent them his cheque in March 1880, but the Building Acts Committee and the Board of Works raised various objections. Carte wrote in a letter to *The Times*[2] "I am drowning in the meshes of red tape." He listed the six stages that the plan already had to pass through, followed by another five – to culminate in the Lord Chamberlain's office. Carte added "This is always supposing that I have not in the interval been driven to lunacy or suicide." On 4 June 1880, and following further objections, the Board gave its agreement.

Two days earlier, Emden posed another problem. He had originally quoted £12,000 for building. On 2 June 1880 he told Carte that the lowest possible cost would be £18,000. Carte thought the revised price was too high, and ordered Emden to stop building. He dismissed Emden on 8 June. Emden sued for Carte for £1,490 for services already rendered, plus £3,000 for wrongful dismissal. Emden abandoned his case in November 1881.

Carte was then free to engage another architect. This time his choice was as suitable as Emden had been unsuitable. Charles John Phipps had already been the architect for 11 theatres. His first major work was rebuilding (1862–63) the Theatre Royal, in his native city of Bath. The theatre had been destroyed by fire, and he placed high priority on fire safety in his work. Before the

1. Much information in this chapter was taken from *The Savoyard*, September 1981, pages 4–7
2. The Times, 22 May 1880

Savoy he was responsible for six London theatres – Queen's Theatre, Long Acre (1867), Gaiety Theatre, London (1868), Olympic Theatre (1870), Varieties Music Hall, Hoxton (1870) and Vaudeville Theatre, London (1871). In the 1880s critics considered that the Savoy Theatre had 'outdone all the architect's previous work.'

A particular tribute to Phipps came when he was chosen by the Royal Institute of British Architects as architect for their own headquarters at 9 Conduit Street in a very fashionable part of London. This elegant building echoes the 18th and 19th century neo-classical style of Bath's crescents and bridges. Phipps was true to his native city.

The Savoy Theatre opened on 10 October 1881. Already *Patience* had been performed 170 times at the Opéra Comique. The eagerness with which the audience greeted the 171st performance of *Patience* equaled the enthusiasm shown on the other first nights.[3] As the electric lights were switched on, there was a hum of expectation throughout the house. Four men took curtain calls at the end of the performance. They were Gilbert, Sullivan, Richard D'Oyly Carte and C. J. Phipps.[4]

On the opening night of the Savoy Theatre Carte addressed the audience from the stage:

> "From the time, now some years since, that the first electric lights in lamps were exhibited outside the Paris Opera House, I have been convinced that electric light in some form is the light of the future for use in theatres, not to go further."

Helen, with her academic background in Mechanical Philosophy must have particularly welcomed the freedom from gas lamps.

A Star of the show was the electric lighting of stage, back-stage and auditorium. As *Building News* reported, this was the first instance of any public building being lighted permanently in all departments by the electric light. "This has been undertaken by Messrs Siemens & Company and the lights adopted are those adopted are those by Swan of Newcastle, and known as the Swan Incandescent Light." The power needed to generate the electric current for so many lights was supplied by powerful steam engines in a separate building on separate land adjoining the

---

3. Illustrated London News, 16 October 1881
4. Many details are from *The Savoyard* magazine,. Volume 20, number 2, which I edited at the time

THE NEW SAVOY THEATRE, FRONT TOWARDS THE THAMES EMBANKMENT.

theatre. The lights were beautifully coloured and in no way impaired the atmosphere of the theatre. They emitted no heat and were not of the piercing brightness seen from lamps on the streets. There were about 1,200 lights in the theatre. When Helen was interviewed by her brother in Chapter 9, she drew attention to absence of heat in the gridiron above the stage.

Carte announced his new theatre in a letter to the *Daily Telegraph* in 1881. "On the Savoy manor there was formerly a theatre. I have used the ancient name as an appropriate title for the present one."

The Savoy Theatre had 1292 seats. There were 18 excellent private boxes. The theatre was built without pillars, ensuring a clear, unobstructed view from every seat. The interior design, by Collinson & Lock was revolutionary in that it provided an austere and disciplined setting for the operas. Simple Renaissance plaster modeling was shaded in tones of white, yellow and gold – an

absolute contrast to the hordes of cherubims, angels and partially drawn ladies that were modeled on the walls and ceilings of other theatres of the day. Instead of the usual act-drops, there was a gold-coloured curtain. Gilbert had a clear idea of how the operas should be presented; he saw them as 'operas of repose.' The Savoy was the first theatre with an environment conducive to repose.

Phipps made a virtue of the fact that the Savoy was built on a sloping site. Because it was built on an island site, all parts of the theatre could be easily accessible. Ease of access was further enhanced by having the entrance to the Upper Circle and the Gallery from the Strand. The Dress Circle, Stalls and Pit were reached from the Embankment.

Leslie Baily quotes two reports on the impact of the electrical lighting on the first night. The *Electrical Times* said:

"When the curtain fell, Mr D'Oyly Carte came on grasping an electric lamp and a hush fell upon the audience, who thought that electricity was always fatal. He then delighted them with a sort of polytechnic lecture à la Professor Pepper, respecting the safety of the electric light in a theatre. Finally he placed a piece of muslin round the lamp and held it up as who would say 'You see there is no deception.' He then took a hammer and smashed the lamp, which naturally went out. But when he held up the muslin unburnt the effect on the audience was electric, in both senses of the word. D'Oyly Carte heard enthusiastic cheers, which were so prolonged that he had to go on and take two calls".

Baily also quotes a report from *The Continental Times*, showing how widespread were the implications for theatres worldwide. This extract is dated Geneva, 29 October 1881.

"The striking novelties and undreamt of improvements at the Savoy Theatre were greeted by a crowded audience of London's elect with every visible and audible sign of enthusiastic approval. Mr Carte was summoned before the curtain to receive public recognition of his enterprising spirit and admirable taste. The chief success of course was the unquestionable triumph of the electric light, conclusively proved to be susceptible of discipline and not a whit less manageable than its forerunner, the malodorous, scorching, blinding, oxygen-consuming coal gas, doomed, I hope and believe, to speedy extinction. Swan, by inventing the incandescent lamp, and D'Oyly Carte, by adapting it to his splendid theatrical venue, have paved the way for the application of electricity to the lighting of private houses, and those meritorious achievements may without exaggeration be held to entitle them to the gratitude of civilized humanity."

The Savoy was the first London theatre to be built according to the requirements of the Fire Act of 1878. It showed a greater concern for safety than ever before. All parts of the theatre had at least two exits. The stage was completely separated from the auditorium by a brick wall going right up to the roof. All entrances, passages and staircases were made of fire-resistant materials. The fire hydrants were of a new, improved form, with the new Metropolitan Brigade gauge thread that enabled boxes to be connected more rapidly. It was the first time that the thread had been used for any private building. I carried out additional research at the time when the centenary issue of *The Savoyard* was being written. From October 1880 to October 1881 The Era reported frequent meetings at Carte's offices with Eyre Massey Shaw, Superintendent of the Metropolitan Fire Brigade, Shaw was not only a brave firefighter, he was also an influential thinker on firefighting, publishing at least one book on the subject. He advised Carte on the layout of the theatre, the fire-resistant materials to use and the arrangements to ensure that everyone could exit the theatre within a few minutes.

The positioning of the theatre made it possible to construct a virtually private road. Outside a 70 foot covered way allowed six or seven private carriages to arrive simultaneously.

Carte had high standards about what the Savoy audience should expect when they purchased tickets. He established the first ever queuing system, replacing the hurly-burly whereby the strongest got the seats and the weakest did not even get as far as the wall. Ticket vouchers were printed with seating plans on the back. The first theatrical programmes as we know them today were printed for audiences at the Savoy Theatre. They were a great improvement on the old crudely printed playbills. They were issued free of charge. Whisky served in the theatre bars was <u>real</u> whisky. Coffee was <u>real</u> coffee, not chicory. Carte also abolished the custom of tipping the attendants.

Helen was not at the Savoy for its electrical First Night on 10 October 1881. She was managing the New York production of *Patience* at the Standard Theater, which had opened on 22 September 1881. This followed the pattern set by the New York production of *The Pirates of Penzance*. J. H. Ryley, who had previously played Major General Stanley now played Bunthorne, *Patience* at the Standard Theater achieved 177 performances, closing on 23 March 1882.

Iolanthe is unique among the Savoy Operas in that its premiere productions in London and New York took place on the same day, 25 November 1882. Helen managed the New York production at the Fifth Avenue Theater. Carte wrote to her warning about the risk of upsetting the censor in England –

> If ever it gets over to the Lord Chamberlain's office that the sacred orders of the Garter, Thistle, Patrick and Bath are going on the stage, the office may come down hang and prevent it being done.[5]

Following the death of Richard D'Oyly Carte on 3 April 1901, Helen inherited sole responsibility for the staging of the operas. The first Savoy opera that she chose to revive was *Iolanthe*, from 7 December 1901 to 29 March 1902. *Iolanthe* had a special place in Helen's heart.

Bazalgette's site shown at the start of this chapter gave a superb opportunity to create a prestigious development in what was then the centre of London's theatrical world. First came the

---

5.   *The Gilbert and Sullivan Book* Leslie Baily. Cassell & Co 1952. Page 168

Embankment Gardens in 1874; Carte opened the Savoy Theatre in 1881. A substantial area of land remained undeveloped. The north east corner, which fronted on to the Strand, presented an unimpressive, higgeldy piggeldy amalgam of shops, offices and workshops.

Helen had seen that in New York high-class hotels were an integral part of the theatrical life. The novelist Compton Mackenzie, in *The Savoy of London*, was an admirer of Helen's contribution[6].

> "D'Oyly Carte's second wife must be given much of the credit for the achievement of the Savoy Theatre and the Savoy Hotel. She was Helen Couper Black, a daughter of the procurator-fiscal of Wigtownshire... After taking a brilliant degree at London University, she went on the stage as Helen Lenoir. Then she became D'Oyly Carte's secretary and later his manager. They were married in 1888. She was a devotee of electricity, and everything else that could contribute to the comfort of life. To this day her feminine hand is discernible in the atmosphere of the Savoy, which combines grandeur with homeliness, luxury with simplicity, and good taste with comfort

Another innovation in which perhaps Mrs Carte's hand may be traced was the continuous service on every floor available to guests. This, with the aid of communication by speaking tube from every floor and the installation of service lifts, made every floor at any hour of the day and night a private house, and moreover an extremely well-run private house at that. Indeed, the hotel seemed a vast private house when it was first opened, with its own artesian well bored 420 feet down to reach the pure water in the chalk beds underneath London.

The Savoy's independence from the start – a kind of liberty within the Liberty of the Duchy of Lancaster – allowed its creators to take for granted that the service of a hotel would include such items as lights, baths and attendance, for which – a very conspicuous innovation in 1889 – no extra charge was levied.

Immunity from noise was studied by D'Oyly Carte's architects, builders, and advisers, and this policy has been followed ever since. The increase in street traffic and outside noise in modern times has been met by the installation of double windows and air

6. *The Savoy of London*, Compton Mackenzie, Harrap & Co Ltd, London 1951, pages 44–46.

conditioning. The Savoy also claimed to be the first building in the world (certainly the first in England) constructed of incombustible material throughout. The floors and partitions were of 'cemen concrete', encasing steel joists, and there was practically no wood except doors and window frames. The proportion of the upper floors was not reduced, which was then a novelty. Ceilings were as high on the top floor as on the first. Accommodation was arranged in suites and every suite of two or more rooms had, in addition to its own bathroom, its own w.c. A *private* w.c. seems to have been a luxury unheard of before."

The hotel of course was on the same site as the Savoy Theatre, and the risks of fire, smoke inhalation and panic had taken a huge toll in theatres throughout the 1800s.

The Savoy Hotel led the way in England in its bathrooms. When the builder Mr Holloway saw there were 70 specified, he asked D'Oyly Carte whether he was expecting his guests to be amphibians.

Helen knew from her experience that hotel guests in New York expected their hotels to provide them with a bathroom, and that this requirement would soon find its way across the Atlantic to London.

The share capital of the Savoy Company, incorporated on 28 May 1889 was £100,000. One of the directors was Michael Gunn whose links with Richard and Helen went all the way back to when he hosted Carte's Comedy Opera Company in *Trial by Jury* and *The Sorcerer* at the Gaiety Theatre Dublin in summer 1878 and who had been the manager of *Aladdin*, the pantomime in which Helen appeared in 1876–7.[7]

7. *The Savoy, the romance of a great hotel* by Stanley Jackson, Frederick Muller & Co, pages 20–21

14

Helen as peacemaker in the Carpet Quarrel

By 1889 the Gilbert and Sullivan operas had become completely associated with the Savoy Theatre. All the works, whether originally produced there or at the Opéra Comique, were known as 'The Savoy Operas', and even Gilbert used the term 'Savoyard' to describe himself and others who had worked there. The relationships within the partnership, however, had started to deteriorate. A series of disagreements, culminating in what became known as the Carpet Quarrel led to its dissolution. Sullivan and Carte continued in partnership and the Savoy was used for works other than those by Gilbert and Sullivan.

Helen was involved with the Quarrel from the start. She never, at any stage, lost the respect and respect of W. S. Gilbert. It was Helen's skill as a peacemaker that eventually achieved a truce. Without Helen's calming influence, it is unlikely that *Utopia Limited* and *The Grand Duke* would ever have been written and composed.

The premier of *The Gondoliers* at the Savoy Theatre on 7 December 1889 was rapturously received by the London public and the critics. Over a thousand people applied for seats on the first night. Gilbert and Sullivan were called to take a curtain call. Carte too was called. Gilbert wrote to Sullivan on the following day – "it gives me the chance of shining through the twentieth century with a reflected light.'" Sullivan replied "Don't talk of reflected light. In such a brilliant book as *The Gondoliers* you shine with an individual brilliancy which no other writer can hope to attain."[1] So everyone appeared to be happy.

---

1. *W.S. Gilbert a classic Victorian and his theatre.* Jane Stedman, Oxford University Press, New York 1996, p266-289

The New York production of *The Gondoliers* opened at the Park Theatre on 7 January 1890. Early in November Helen had assured Gilbert that she would "leave no stone unturned to send a good company"[2] Perhaps what *The Gondoliers* really needed was a good press agent like Colonel Morse who had helped to 'sell' the earlier operas to the New York critics. When Carte and Helen arrived in New York on 26 January, adverse criticism had already done severe damage.

On 20 December Gilbert had taken his wife Kitty on a touring holiday to India. He was interested in India as a possible setting for his next opera and Kitty had lived in India when her father had been posted there as a British officer. Carte told Gilbert that *The Gondoliers* was not doing well in New York. From Agra Gilbert wrote to Carte

> "I am sorry for that but it's a very difficult piece to cast properly so I confess I was not very sanguine. I found *The Mikado* and *Trial by Jury* playing in Calcutta – it seems our pieces are continually played there and it seems monstrous that we have no agent to protect our interest."

This letter was business-like and affable.

Gilbert and Kitty came back to London at the start of April 1890. The first hint of trouble came when Kitty told Gilbert that she had seen that Barrington as Giuseppe was putting in unauthorized gags. Gilbert wrote to Carte

> "The piece is, I think, good enough without the extraneous embellishments suggested by Mr Barrington's brief fancy, anyway it must be played <u>exactly as I wrote it.</u> I won't have an outside word introduced by anyone. If once a licence in this direction is accorded it opens the door to any amount of tomfoolery."

Gilbert had long been frustrated by Sullivan's wish to write serious music. This showed, for example, by the way that Sullivan was performing *The Golden Legend* when Gilbert wanted him to concentrate on *Ruddygore*. Another distraction came with the building of the Royal English Opera House.

Helen had laid the foundation stone. She and Richard had good reason to expect the same success that followed the opening of the Savoy Theatre. The opening with Sullivan's *Ivanhoe* did not take

2. *Gilbert and Sullivan a dual biography,* Michael Ainger, OUP, New York 2002, p 395-397

place until 31 January 1891, but Gilbert felt that the venture had distracted Sullivan from *The Gondoliers*, though he did not blame Helen for laying the first stone.

The Royal English Opera House should have been a success. Carte had acquired a superb site in Cambridge Circus. London's theatre land had centered on the Strand in the 1870s, but the focus for musical theatre was quickly moving west. New theatres were being built in and around Shaftesbury Avenue, which is the street on the left of the picture.

Carte had engaged a most eminent architect, Thomas Edward Collcutt. The Prince of Wales (later Edward VII) greatly approved Collcutt's design for the Imperial Institute. Carte had a highly respected English librettist in Julian Sturgis.

But no English opera composer was available, Carte instead turned to André Messager who had in 1894 composed *Mirette*, which turned out to achieve the shortest run of any Savoy opera. In place of *Ivanhoe* Messager came up with *La Basoche*, which had already appeared in Paris some 11 years earlier. The basoche was a guild of Parisian law clerks. It ran for just over two months.

Gilbert may well have approved of Collcutt because he had originally trained in the office of Richard Norman Shaw, and Shaw was the man who designed Grim's Dyke, Gilbert's magnificent stately home near Harrow. But storm clouds were gathering.

Immediately after the first performance of *The Gondoliers*, Gilbert was in a positive mood. As we have seen at the start of this chapter, Gilbert wrote to Sullivan the morning after opening night

> "I must thank you for the magnificent work you have put into the piece. It gives one the chance of shining right through the twentieth century with a reflected light."

Carte informed Gilbert that the preliminary expenses of *The Gondoliers* were £4500. Astounded, Gilbert asked Carte for details. Carte's resumé included over £100 for the dresses of Decima Moore as Casilda and £100 for the second dress of Rosina Brandram as the Duchess. What surprised Gilbert most of all was £500 for new carpets for the front of the house. There was no verbatim record of who said what to whom at a meeting of Gilbert, Sullivan and Carte, but Helen said "I am sure you are not thinking what you were saying, Mr Gilbert." She thought him strangely violent and insulting. In fact Gilbert was suffering from an attack of gout, and that probably made matters even worse.

Quarter day for distribution of the profits came on 4 July, but Carte withheld them on his solicitor's advice. On 30 July Gilbert issued a writ for his share, which he estimated as at least £3,000. Carte sent £2,000. Gilbert's solicitor advised him to move for receivership. Carte's counsel objected to Gilbert's 'cruel conduct'. Carte was ordered to pay Gilbert £1,000 the next day and to produce the year's accounts within three weeks.

Thereafter there was an uneasy truce. Carte offered Gilbert seats for the first anniversary of *The Gondoliers* on 7 December 1890. Carte and Gilbert had publicly shaken hands, but Gilbert did not go to the performance. Hostility remained. Carte imagined fresh litigation in every suggestion by Gilbert, and Gilbert saw a fresh insult in Carte's every response.

To Helen goes the credit for the eventual collaboration in *Utopia Ltd* (1893) and *The Grand Duke* (1896). Gilbert liked and admired Helen... Only Helen could bring about the eventual reconciliation.

15

Helen as planner & 'Great White Mother' in the 1890s

Carte and Helen had gone to New York on 7 January 1890 to save the ailing production of *The Gondoliers*. Their determination is shown by the fact that a passenger list shows they did not come back to England until 5 March 1890. The list shows they were accompanied by a valet[1].

High points for the company were the two command performances of *The Gondoliers* (Windsor 6 March 1891) where Jessie Bond claimed she sat on Queen Victoria's chair, and *The Mikado* (Balmoral 1891) where George Thorne showed off his comic skills as Ko-Ko.

Throughout the 1890s the records show Carte consistently suffered bouts of bad health. Helen's care and affection helped to keep him going.

A major highlight for Richard, Helen and everyone, front and back stage in C Company came on Friday 4 September 1891. *The Mikado* was played at Balmoral as a Royal Command Performance for Queen Victoria. George Thorne the great touring comedian played Ko-Ko and Fred Billington was Pooh-Bah.

There was a patchy repertoire of shows produced at the Savoy Theatre between *The Gondoliers* (closed 20 June 1891) and *The Grand Duke* (opened 7 March 1896). The first show was *The Nautch Girl* (30 June 1891 20 performances). It was written by Frank Desprez and George Dance, with music by Edward Solomon. Desprez had been on Carte's staff with Helen when she first joined Carte in 1876.

---

1. Passenger list White Star Line New York to Liverpool

The Vicar of Bray[2] by Sidney Grundy and Edward Solomon (2 July 1892 141 performances) achieved a respectable run. It had Rutland Barrington in the title role and Barrington continued to be a great favourite with the Savoy audiences.

Grundy also wrote *Haddon Hall* (24 September 1892 204 performances). Sullivan wrote the music. Next came *Jane Annie* or *The Good-Conduct Prize* (13 May 1893 50 performances). The librettists were J. M. Barrie and Arthur Conan Doyle. Despite the fame of these two writers in other fields *The Good-Conduct Prize* was not a success. Conan Doyle wrote to Helen on 17 December 1902 from his home at 12 Tennison Road, South Norwood to say that he agreed with the admirable criticism that she had raised with Mr Barrie, and that by Monday they would be ready for a meeting. It is interesting that the letter was written nearly five months before the eventual premier production. The Savoy went dark for three months afterwards.

Jeffrey Snelson (Jeoffry Theodore Hewett Snelson) appeared in the juvenile role of Caddie in *Jane Annie*, and later created Pedrillo, the goatherd, in *The Chieftain*. He is a child of the Hewett/Hollingsworth family mentioned in Chapter 5 of this book. His sister Tessa (Theresa Mary Hewett Snelson) had been engaged as a chorister for the Savoy in 1892 and toured with E Company from 1894.

The penultimate opera in the partnership was launched on 7 October 1893. An interview published on that same day as the premier of *Utopia Ltd* casts light on the importance of Helen in the success of the operas.[3]

The picture is fascinating. Left to right the people are Mrs Gilbert, François Cellier, Sullivan, Gilbert, Helen and Richard D'Oyly Carte, W H Denny, Emmie Owen, Florence Perry, C Harris,

---

2. Barrington cartoon from *Ally Sloper's Half Holiday* 27 February 1892, page 67
3. *The Graphic* 7 October 1893, page 450

W H Seymour, Rutland Barrington, Rosina Brandram, Nancy McIntosh, Lawrence Gridley, Charles Kenningham, Scott Fishe and Walter Passmore. The principal performers sit facing the management. Gilbert insisted that they all listened attentively, and he did not tell them whom he was casting for which role until he had finished reading the whole libretto. We see Nancy McIntosh among the cast. Gilbert was planning that she should take the leading soprano role of Princess Selene. She had little experience of singing principal roles in musical works and none at all of singing in the Savoy operas.

An extract from an interview in The Graphic shortly before the first night of Utopia Ltd shows the importance of Helen within the management of the company at this time:

A CHAT WITH MR AND MRS D'OYLY CARTE
There is, therefore, an interval of ten minutes, which the ladies of the chorus devote to calling in Art to the aid of Nature, and in which Sir Arthur chats to his friends in the boxes. Mr D'Oyly Carte returns to his stage box and to his correspondence. Usually, he watches the rehearsals and writes at the same time. He suffers many interruptions and the presence of an admirer more or less does not ruffle him in the least.

"I can talk and write as well, if you don't mind," he says, "but, really, you ought not to question me, but Mrs Carte. She's the business woman, and she really can do two things at a time – six, I believe. She will be down here in a moment."

The scratch of the pen accompanies Mr D'Oyly Carte's remarks.

"We're getting near the end of the rehearsals now, you see. It is not till this week that they're so complete. You see, we haven't the band yet; all the rehearsals go to the piano. The band is practised separately at St Andrew's Hall. On Tuesday and Wednesday the voices are tried with the band – still at St Andrew's Hall and for the music only. On Thursday and Friday we have full-dress rehearsals, On Saturday – 'Comes at last the final stroke'.

A knock on the door and an interruption – a welcome one for it is Mrs D'Oyly Carte. "Mrs Carte," pursues Mr Carte, "will tell you all about the early rehearsals."

"They are very different from these," says Mrs Carte, "because it is only at this stage that all the component parts come together. They begin six or seven weeks beforehand with the music only. The music is learned by heart first, and Sir Arthur rehearses the band by itself. Then Mr Gilbert reads the play to the company, and the parts are given out. It isn't until the fifth week of rehearsals that dialogue and songs begin to go together. You see, things have to be altered to meet the needs of the case. For instance, in the beginning Sir Arthur and Mr Gilbert make mutual concessions, the one altering the music to fit the songs, and the other adapting the songs to go with the music; and the scenery – although a model of the *tout ensemble* is made at first – is continually altered to fit the grouping and provide for the exits and the entrances."

"Do you keep the same chorus from opera to opera?"

"Well, we can hardly do that," she replies. "They are bound to change a great deal; but they change less than the principals. Let me see who are left – well, there's Mr Barrington and Miss Brandram – I think they've been here since the first, and Mr Denny has been a long time; but this is an unusually 'new' company.

"I have often wondered how you 'cast' your companies."

"Well, of course, so far as the principals are concerned, that is a matter of special arrangement; but so far as the choruses, there is no difficulty in finding these. Since Mr Carte began these operas with *The Sorcerer* in 1877, we have accumulated 7,000 names on our books, with the voice, the appearance, and the ability of each lady and gentleman carefully catalogued.

"But 7,000, Mrs Carte – what can you do with them?"

"Well, you see," said Mrs Carte, "we have five provincial companies now. A provincial company of *Utopia Limited* itself will be sent out in about six weeks. And another at Christmas."

"Mrs D'Oyly Carte hasn't told you," said Mr Carte, "that it is she who manages these companies, arranges all the dates, all the bookings – we are booked to the end of 1894 – and every other detail of organisation. I have an idea that she does it with some kind of conjuring and a 'Bradshaw[4]'."

"You generally have a company in America?"

"Not now," said Mr Carte, who, by the way, has no high opinion of some of the American managers, "though I prefer to send my own companies out. If you sell an American manager the rights he is apt to introduce innovations. They introduced a ballet into one of the operas, and in the *Pinafore* they had girls for the sailors."

As we watched Mr Gilbert still anxiously directing, still polishing to the pattern his own design the smallest detail, it was rather interesting to speculate upon his possible state of mind if he saw a ballet introduced into *The Yeomen of the Guard*. He was out of reach of such disturbing reflections here, being engaged, in fact, with a Mistress of Deportment in idealising the curtseys of the ladies of the chorus. "A little lower down and spread the train," said the Mistress of the Deportment. "Spread each other's trains, ladies!" echoed Mr Gilbert (and we could hear Mr Charles Harris inquiring sarcastically of some of the ladies nearest to him if they imagined they were laying a table-cloth); "And slide the feet, ladies! Oh, slide the feet" Continues Madame X, with an unconscious reminiscence of the hard case of Mr Bultitude.[5]

"Mr Gilbert seems rather anxious," I said, "It must be rather a trial to him on first nights."

"He never comes," said Mr Carte. "Sir Arthur Sullivan and myself are present; but Mr Gilbert generally walks on the Embankment. Last time he spent the evening at the Gaiety."

---

4. Bradshaw railway timetables were the universally recognised guide for travellers.
5. Mr Bultitude was in Charles Dickens's *Oliver Twist*.

Initials at the end of the interview show that it was conducted by ESG.

Shortly after *Utopia Ltd* finished, the next production was Mirette with music by André Messager and libretto by Harry Greenbank and Fred Weatherly. This ran for 41 performances from 3 July to 11 August 1894. A revised version ran for 61 performances from 6 October to 6 December 1894.

Sullivan came back for the next production. *The Chieftain* ran for 97 performances from 12 December 1894 to 16 March 1895. The cast was rich in established Savoyards – it included Courtice Pounds, Walter Passmore, Richard Temple, Scott Russell, Florence Perry, Emmie Owen, Scott Fishe and Rosina Brandram, as well as Florence St. John. Despite this glittering cast and Sullivan's reputation *The Chieftain* closed at the Savoy after only 97 performances. The company then toured for about a month from 18 March. The Carl Rosa Company leased the Savoy from 16 April to 15 June. They presented *Hansel and Gretel* by Engelbert Humperdinck. The Savoy then remained closed until 6 November.

Much credit for the wisdom of the next choice must go to Helen. A revival of *The Mikado* opened on 6 November 1895 and achieved 127 performances by 4 March 1896. A full array of Savoyards appeared. Sullivan conducted on the first night and the cast list included Barrington, Passmore, Kenningham, Scott Fishe, Rosina Brandram and Jessie Bond.

The stage was set, well and truly, for the premiere of *The Grand Duke* on 7 March 1896. Sullivan again conducted on the first night and a full array of Savoyards took part. However, *The Grand Duke* closed on 10 July 1896 after only 123 performances. This was the shortest run of any of Carte's Gilbert and Sullivan operas. The weakness of *The Grand Duke* was confirmed by the fact that six matinees from 27 May to 4 July were of *The Mikado*.

The Hungarian actress Ilka Palmay[6] was recruited to play Julia Jellicoe in *The Grand Duke*. Helen helped her settle into the part and Ilka Palmay remembered Helen in a biographic article.[7]

> "My husband wanted to hear nothing of me devoting myself – and permanently to my profession but he could not prevent me giving me giving serious consideration to a surprise invitation of the Savoy Theatre relating to three years at a high and increasing salary and accompanied by

6. She was listed at the Savoy as Ilka von Palmay but she used von only briefly.
7. The Gilbert and Sullivan Journal, translation by Andrew Lamb September 1972, pages 417–419, 439–440

the more flattering assurance that England's Johann Strauss and his librettist Gilbert, one of the most distinguished librettists, would write an operetta for me in which I would play a foreigner so that my foreign accent would be well motivated, if not a necessity".

What to do? What to do in the face of such invitation? The Savoy Theatre was at that time the premier stage in Britain after Covent Garden and I dare say the most high-class. So for example no lady had set foot on the boards of the theatre either in stockinette or in male costume for it was considered not at all comme il faut. British operas in particular did not achieve performance here by reason of their obscurity. Just as it is customary with us to bring out gay, currently popular stage works on the walls of the theatre building, so here one found everywhere – even in all the wardrobes –theatre regulations on the cardinal rules of the house. Here is just something from the Draconian statute. On pain of instant dismissal all obscene talk and any such act was forbidden in every room of the house. These articles had for years always been followed so conscientiously and strictly that a high-class mode of thinking and living was instilled into the flesh and blood of everyone belonging to the Savoy Theatre without exception down to the most modest member of the chorus.

The members of the company are so placed with their salaries that they are able to cover the necessities of life handsomely. So belonging to the Savoy Theatre in itself bestows a certain social status and secures esteem in the big cities.

My husband too could find no realistic objection to this theatre's offer and the request of the aforementioned authors. So immediately I drew up the contract. Sullivan and Gilbert promised to send me the role and the music in good time, and then I travelled back as an English soubrette on our small Carinthian estate where I learned the language of Shakespeare with my English companion at double speed.

At last the long-awaited role arrived. I scarcely understood the libretto which was written in Gilbert's style, and even for Englishwomen presented some riddles and had some difficulties in store. So I learned the role, which throughout contained spirited versions, in parrot fashion. Every syllable that demanded a stronger accent my English friend underlined for me, and in this way I studied the role literally syllable by syllable. At four o'clock in the morning I started learning by heart and carried on until eight o'clock. At ten I recited everything I had taken in early on. After lunch I wrote out English and read aloud. I could, I suppose, say that this study was real torture. Often I fainted from exhaustion. Then when I regained consciousness I asked the companion to say nothing about it to my husband and worked on in the same way. For once I had committed myself to something and started on it, it could not present sufficiently strong obstacles for me to abandon it by calling a halt halfway.

People say that I possess a quite special talent for picking up foreign languages. That is correct only with qualifications. My unlimited zeal was decisive. For had I not learned German no less than English with such cast-iron application and with daily renewed energy I would not have attained the proficiency in those two languages to be able to obtain recognition and fame in Vienna and Berlin as a German actress and in London on one of the premier stages in an English role.

As autumn approached we journeyed to London again. We took with us a quantity of small requirements which would help us soon feel at home abroad. Our cook too, the manservant and two pet dogs accompanied us over there. On arrival we put up first at the Victoria Hotel, but at once set out looking for somewhere to live. We were lucky, found a charming little house in Dover Street and rented it. Then we paid our visit to the manager of the Savoy Theatre, Mr d'Oly. He was the boss of three theatre companies, the one worked in London, the second (Touring Company) was travelling in the provinces; the third was playing in Australia, at Sydney. And these three troupes were commanded, not by the man himself, who was half paralysed from a stroke, but by a lady, his wife – a woman whom one describe as plain rather than beautiful. As I later learned, she had, when the manager was still fit, been engaged by him as a chorus girl, advanced later to office secretary and finally to all-powerful lady manager. She was acknowledged as a genial person and lived only for work. She had no family; so that she loved animals all the more fondly, especially dogs. She owned a large dog of truly human intelligence which she called her best friend.

Having quickly discovered that she was a dog-lover, I told the lady manager that I had brought with me two nice dogs, one of which had been ill on the sea journey. She expressed profound sympathy – I was told later that she took such a swift and hearty liking to me because, like her, I was a dog-lover – and since her four-footed adjutant was also ailing just then, our conversation turned more on dogs' ailments than my new role. She also sent me at once to the vet, but he was unfortunately unable to give any more help. Despite all his careful directions and careful nursing, both dogs died. I mourned my little Missy, though to be sure not so grief-stricken as Mrs d'Oly who for her departed darling had a double-lined coffin made, and had it brought to her estate and buried there. For a long time after she could speak of her 'best friend' only with tears in her eyes.

For the purpose of studying the role, Gilbert invited me for a week to his manor house situated near London where he and his wife entertained me as lovingly as if I had been a member of the family. The following week I was the guest of Sullivan, who owned a delightful villa on the banks of the Thames.

There is nothing remarkable that on English stages they play without a prompter. The mass of rehearsals make that natural. First countless solo rehearsals take place, followed by musical rehearsals on the stage at which everyone, music in hand, sings his part seated. Then rehearsals of the libretto are first held. And only when both have settled down – do music and words for the full rehearsals begin, and they continue, day in, day out for about two months."

In addition to Helen's work at the Savoy, she played a big part in managing the touring companies. These companies were important because they brought the operas to small towns such as Preston, Dudley and Tunbridge Wells in Kent. They provided additional profits. Lindsay Harman, who spent eleven years with D'Oyly Carte, mainly with E Company, sang in the chorus, played small parts and made occasional understudy appearances. This picture shows Harman as Bill Bobstay in *HMS Pinafore*. His first contract had taken him to New York where he was in the chorus of *The Gondoliers*. Another high spot was the command performance of *The Mikado* for Queen Victoria at Balmoral in 1891. Harman's reminiscences give an account of life in the touring companies and how they were managed. There are anecdotes and letters and telegrams about how Helen related to them.[8] Harman, like Helen, had a particular affection for E Company:

"I often look back on those days and think of the happy life of a chorister, free from responsibility and not worrying about his voice being a bit off colour. It was about this time that I went on for my first part, viz as Pish Tush in *The Mikado* at the Royalty Theatre, Glasgow – this was in 1891. (C Company who played the Command Performance at Balmoral was in Glasgow for four weeks in1891 – January 19 & 26: August 10 & 17). I little knew then that I was destined later to play the part for over three years. I presume that it was on account of my being found useful and a quick study that I was drafted to the E Company to understudy the leading parts and play some small ones.

The companies were called A, B, C, D, E, etc. This did not, however, signify that A Company was the first or more important; in fact, it was just the reverse. It depended upon one's self to a great extent whether one was happy in the company. However the management had a great deal to answer for; one can realize that a bully of a stage manager, or an autocratic musical director, could make life somewhat unpleasant, and as members of different companies were in touch we knew what was going on. This accounted for a little quotation the 'boys' used in the dressing rooms, which was appropriate at the time. It is from *The Mikado* and will be easily recognised –

A is happy, oh so happy, laughing Ha! Ha!

Is B more worthy etc

Also from the *Yeomen* Is the little E (ase) sufficiently uncomfortable?

Grievances were always most patiently enquired into by Mrs Carte and I think she must have known the personal history of half of her people. 'I shall write and tell Mrs Carte'

---

8.   A Comic Opera Life by Lindsay Harman, William Barlow, Exeter Street, London, 1924

was constantly heard. Even their domestic troubles were made as an excuse for writing to the 'office'. On this account poor Walter Summers used to playfully allude to the 'Great White Mother'; there was one thing, however, the management at headquarters strongly objected to; that was being worried with telegrams; these were ignored. I recall to mind a couple of instances, though, where wires brought replies. One was from a chorister who was understudy for the principal tenor. His message ran 'Rackstraw off tonight, X— being put on, who am I? G— T—.'[9] Reply: 'Don't know: who are you?' Oh, those tenors! The other was from a stage manager. He had become impatient with a soprano who had been sent to join the company. So his lordship wired 'Prima donna no good, send another. F— L—.'[10] The return message ran 'Rehearse the lady and mind your own business' Another 'You say we shall hear from you shortly; as <u>short</u> as you please'.

One member, wishing to air a grievance, thought he would 'steal a march' on the touring management and 'get one in' first. He accordingly caught the midnight train to town. Unable to get nearer the sanctum than the outer office, he had to content himself with an interview with Mr H— the secretary. Asked on his return to the company how he found the gentleman, he replied 'placid, sir, placid – he's pick his teeth whilst his house was burning if the fire started after dinner.' The method of trying to steal a march on the local management seldom resulted to the advantage of the individual 'trying it on'. The reverse was generally the case, for leaving the company without permission was, in itself, strictly against the rules.

Reverting to myself. I left the C for the E and was then destined to be connected with it for many years. In fact, with the exception of a few breaks, including another American visit, and a couple of short tours with A and D Companies, I was practically a member until I severed my connection with the D'Oyly Carte management, a period of over eleven years with various companies, with an occasional 'show' at the Savoy, which I shall allude to later.

I think it was the last night of the tour, before I left for the E that the gentlemen of the chorus had been accused by the powers that be of being a bit festive. They were highly

9. Most probably Joseph Greene Taylor, chorister and understudy 1888–1892 at least
10. Fred Leon long-time stage manager

indignant but made up their minds to play up to the accusation. When the heralds, pages and pikemen made their entrance (Act II of *The Gondoliers*) titters began to go around the house until they matured into hearty laughter. The Ducal party made their entrance, wondering why they were greeted thus, until the Duke caught sight of the corner page with a very red nose and, looking round, found all his attendants similarly made up. He quickly entered into the joke, went round and warmed his hands at their noses. By the time the stage manager, the late James Scanlan, had made a note of the names of the gentlemen, and a threat of a fine of five shillings each was met with complacency, for the 'boys' had already 'touched' and it was the last night of the tour.

While on the subject I must relate another incident where the boys were carpeted. I forget what the occasion was but they had evidently spent a pleasant day but alcoholic day, and although they had gone through the performance all right, the stage manager J— G—[11] kept them after the fall of the curtain and sent for the business manager Daddy M—[12]. The latter was a man of the world and broad-minded. He asked the stage manager what the complaint was told that one or two fellows had been a bit 'elevated' at the commencement of the performance. 'Well' said M—, 'What do you say, gentlemen?'

Billy G—[13] spoke up; Turning to the stage manager, he said 'Mr G—, did we do our business all right?' 'Yes, fairly so' said G— 'but you were slack.' Daddy M— said 'Gentlemen, you hear what your stage manager says, now let's hear it from you' Billy G spoke up: 'Guv'nor' said he, 'Mr G— first accuses us of being tight, then of being slack, and it's quite evident we couldn't have been both. We'll plead guilty to the latter.'

Daddy laughed and said Billy ought to have been a QC. 'Now Mr G— 'said he 'you accuse them of being slack and they plead guilty; so you have your remedy, call them for rehearsal in the morning and <u>make them tight</u>.'

There's a little anecdote of one member I can't resist. Mr Fred Billington, who played Pooh-Bah in *The Mikado*, was known throughout the country to playgoers, but in

---

11. Probably John Gunn
12. Probably George F Marler Business Manager 1893–1896
13. Probably long-serving chorister William Greatback

describing the following incident it is necessary to recall the elephantine appearance of this portly gentleman. It happened one night after a performance at the Gaiety Theatre, Dublin. 'Billy' called a cab, and was just about to enter it when the stage manager Mr J Scanlan invited him into his, saying that he was passing Billington's hotel and would drop him on his way. The offer was accepted so Billy tipped his own cabby a shilling, saying he would not require him. The cabby scratched his head and hoped his honour would give him more than a shilling. "What, you scamp," said Billy. "But consider the fright your honour put into me and the old horse," said Pat.

Rather more subtle than the London cabby's remark after two stout old gentlemen got out of the 'growler' in the Strand. The same amount was tendered to the cabby – evidently all that he was entitled to. Cabby held it in his palm and soliloquised, loud enough for bystanders to hear as the gentlemen moved off – "Gawd blimey, a tanner a ton!".

It cannot be of the least interest to readers to hear of the various towns and cities, and of my own individual engagements: suffice it to say I have visited all the towns and cities of Great Britain, besides experiencing two American visits, and if I allude at all to any of them it will be for the sake of anecdote or reminiscence. In fact, I can only give an extended string of events extending over a great many years. I have kept no diary and the only records are 'day bills', photographs and press cuttings. So, as I ramble on I expect incidents will often be recalled that happened prior to the one I am relating but it will be a constant case of 'and that reminds me.

This company, I think, established a record of its kind. It was named the E (verlasting) by the boys. You will understand why when I tell you it ran for about seven years without a vacation. A month's holiday was, I believe, the longest during the course of its existence. It was on tour summer and winter, and was essentially a repertoire company. The repertoire was not necessarily large, not more than four operas at a time. When a new opera was produced at the Savoy and we took it up, one of the other works would be dropped for the run of the new one, which would probably be for several months on its own. Then, as business became slack, one of the old works was added and the repertoire gradually built up again. During the years I was with the company we played the following operas: *The*

Mikado, The Gondoliers, Iolanthe, The Sorcerer, Patience, HMS Pinafore, Utopia Limited, The Grand Duke, (The Grand Duchess (Offenbach), *Haddon Hall* (Grundy & Sullivan), *The Rose of Persia* (Hood and Sullivan), *The Vicar of Bray* (Hood & Sullivan), *The Lucky Star, Billy Taylor* (Solomon & Grundy), *Mirette* (Messager), *The Chieftain* and minor works for 'front' pieces such as *Trial by Jury, Captain Billy, After All* etc. We might drop a work for a year or so and revive it again, with others, when business dropped off with our usual repertoire.

When a new opera was to be produced, we rehearsed on tour in the daytime, playing at night from the current repertoire. The producer came down from London, with sometimes author and composer. All scenery and costumes were despatched direct from town and, when ready, all "stuff"' belonging to works we were 'shelving' was returned to headquarters. Great excitement prevailed before the production of a new work as to the cast.

Mr & Mrs Carte would probably come down unknown to members of the company and witness a performance. Nobody knew until after the final curtain that there would probably be a call for full company next morning with an order to bring a song – everybody would be heard sing: understudies would play their parts and a weeding out process would be gone through. Grievances if any would be listened to – manager, stage manager and musical director would be seen with their heads together – 'The Holy Trinity' the boys used to call them. When this trio was in harmony 'God help the rest!' was the saying. 'They'll get their own way.' A cantankerous chorister could be complained about. For example:-

FT[14] a magnificent baritone was a far better singer than the principal, still, it was his duty to understudy,

The conductor, who rejoiced in the Christian name of Mozart, wished a certain phrase sung in a certain way, and Ferdie knew it wasn't good. 'Do as you're told sir, and don't argue, said the conductor. T was stubborn. 'No,' said he. 'I can sing Wagner. I can sing Handel and I can sing Mozart but I'll be hanged if I can sing Mozart W—.

This surely has to be Mozart Wilson.[15]

14. FT Ferdinand Thieler chorister 1882–1887 at least
15. Mozart Wilson was with D'Oyly Carte from 1889–1892

Ilka Palmay played the part of strolling ballad singer Felice in *His Majesty* which opened at the Savoy Theatre on 20 February 1897. Words were by F.C. Burnand, R.C. Lehman and Adrian Ross. Music was by Alexander Mackenzie.

Carte had signed an agreement with them in September 1896. In this opera Ilka sang in German and she performed the nursery rhyme 'Little Miss Muffet' (Das kleine Fräulein Mütchen).

Carte had[16] triumphantly signed George Grossmith who had a huge number of enthusiasts wanting him to come back to the Savoy. Sadly this turned out not to work. Grossmith was tired out from a full programme of his one-man shows. He appeared as Ferdinand V, King of Vingolia only in the first three or four performances. He was replaced by the then inexperienced understudy C.H. Workman. Henry Lytton took over as replacement King Ferdinand on 7 March, but *His Majesty* closed on 24 April, a total of 64 performances.

Fred Billington had created the title role of King Mopolio VII in *His Majesty*. He left the Savoy in April due to illness, and was thus unable to appear as Wilfred Shadbolt in the 1897 revival of *Yeomen* as had been planned, the part going to Henry Lytton instead. This caused some difficulty because Billington was almost twice as heavy as Henry Lytton, so some emergency alterations had to be made and new costumes ordered as soon as possible.

Carte was suffering severe bad health when *His Majesty* premiered on 20 February. Helen did her best to rescue it. She arranged with B Company that Lytton would be released to replace Grossmith as King Ferdinand V. She wrote two long letters to 'Dear G'. First she replied to a telegram from Grossmith saying that he had a cold. Helen knew that Grossmith had a long and expensive contract, she stressed: 'It isn't your fault that you should be ill but it would be your fault if you risked your health and the success of the piece by trying to play before you are strong enough.' In a letter of 3 March Helen pointed out that Grossmith had let himself be trapped in a press interview by saying that his part was not satisfactory. She promised that if she and Carte succeeded in pulling the piece through they would let him have a share of the profits.

Ilka Palmay too had a long and expensive contract. She played Elsie in the revival of *The Yeomen of the Guard* which opened on 3 May 1897 and ran until 20 November. Her participation lasted only until July and she left by mutual consent.

16. Full coverage in *Lytton, Gilbert and Sullivan's Jester* by Brian Jones 2005, pages 80–81

The next opera was *The Grand Duchess of Gerolstein,* composed by Jacques Offenbach. Charles Brookfield and Adrian Ross wrote the libretto, It ran for 104 perform- ances from 4 December 1897 to 12 March 1898. A revival of *The Gondoliers* ran for 104 performances from 22 March to 21 May 1898.

Sullivan composed *The Beauty Stone* with libretto by Arthur Pinero and J Comyns Carr. It opened on 26 May but closed on 16 July after only 50 performances. Helen quickly filled the void by reviving *The Gondoliers,* (18 July to 17 September – 63 performance), then *The Sorcerer* with *Trial by Jury* (22 September to 31 December 1898 – 102 performances). Ivan Caryll's composition of *The Lucky Star* with words by Brookfield, Ross and Hopwood achieved 143 performances (7 January to 31 May 1899).

The century closed with the last opera that Sullivan fully composed, *The Rose of Persia*, with libretto by Basil Hood, ran from (29 November 1899 to 28 June 1900). On 19 December 1899 Helen wrote to Lytton to say that Madame Leon had promised to get a lighter Dervish skirt for his dancing the role of Sultan Mahmoud. Earlier in the 1890s, it was normal for Richard to write, or sign these administrative notes. On 19 December 1899, Helen had to take over even this simple duty.

16

Death of Richard D'Oyly Carte

At the start of the previous chapter, near the cartoon of Barrington in *The Vicar of Bray* it became clear in the 1890s that Richard D'Oyly Carte was a chronically sick man. Helen had taken increasing responsibility for managing the opera company and the Savoy Hotel.

On 7 April 1901 Carte died at their London home, 4 Adelphi Terrace. He was just 27 days short of his 57th birthday. The cause of death was listed as 'dropsy and heart disease'. The medical term is pulmonary oedema. Fluid accumulates in the lungs, leading to impaired gas exchange. In Carte's case it led to heart failure, but it was a protracted process. Helen's love meant that she spent many sleepless nights and anxious days, trying to help him improve his breathing.

The obituaries in the national and theatrical press universally praised Carte for his contribution to English theatre and music. This Ogdens cigarette card is an

unusual testament to the way that Carte was admired by the public.

François Cellier was Carte's musical director at the <u>Opéra Comique</u> and then the Savoy from 1879 to 1902. He gave a detailed account of Carte's relapse when *The Emerald Isle* was presented in April 1900.

> "Although Mr Carte was in too weak a state of health to take any active part in the work of preparation, everybody rejoiced to learn that the patient showed sign; of wonderful improvement, accordingly it was fondly hoped that the esteemed manager's health would be sufficiently restored to allow him to witness the production of the piece. But it was not to be; a few days later Mr Carte had a serious relapse, and his doctor, Sir Thomas Barlow, pronounced him to be in a critical state".[1]

Helen must have known that his life expectancy was limited, but his death came as a severe, devastating shock. Evidence comes in Helen's reply to a letter of condolence that she wrote on 3 May 1901 to Haidee Crofton, who had toured as Hebe in Carte's Comedy Opera Company to Liverpool and Birmingham in April and May 1879. This was the second earliest of Carte's Gilbert and Sullivan tours Carte had taken similar tours to England, Scotland and Ireland in the previous year. Haidee had toured with Carte's companies up to 1891, but only intermittently and never in a Savoy production.

The letter is written from 4 Adelphi Terrace, and signed Helen Carte. It shows Helen's depth of feeling for her long-standing friend.

> "You ask me not to write but I must just thank you for your kind, loving words. I don't know how to write or speak of myself – I am practically dead I don't ask anything now but to be let to go quickly to join him. When I see how his dear old friends – like you – regret his going – I feel they will know a little what it has meant to <u>me</u>. We had got so close through these years of suffering and weakness that of late he was more to me my dearly loved <u>child</u> – my one thing to protect and care for. It is all over now – and I suppose the less I say the better."

1. *Gilbert, Sullivan and D'Oyly Carte* by François Cellier and Cunningham Bridgeman, Sir Isaac Pitman & Sons. London 1914. Pages 373–374.

Helen had sent a telegram to her brother John on 25 March 1901. 'Is mother well? John replied that Mother was quite well. On 9 April John was working as sub-editor of the Express. He saw a report that Richard D'Oyly Carte had died. He contacted his mother and they sent Helen a telegram 'Much sympathy'.[2]

On 5 June John noted in his diary that they had had two or three letters from Helen "She seems very broken-hearted about it all. She does not fix any exact time for coming out as she says she must first obtain probate of the will and pay the various legacies etc."

Helen had been left as sole executrix of Carte's will, and this must have added extra emotional strain during these darkest days. The valuation for probate was £249,817, with a number of small bequests to Savoy staff. All household and personal effects were left to Helen, together with one third of the residuary estate. This must have totaled more than £75,000, so Helen was secure for life.

During the darkest days of Helen's sadness, she continued to manage the Savoy Theatre. During the first revival of *Patience* (7 November 1900 to 20 April 1901 – 150 performances) the Savoy Theatre was closed on four occasions: 22 November 1900 – Sullivan's death 27 November – Sullivan's funeral – 23 January 1901 to 3 February for the death of Queen Victoria and finally 6 April for the death of Richard D'Oyly Carte.

Helen managed the premier production of *The Emerald Isle* or *The Caves* of *Carrig-Cleena* which opened at the Savoy on 27 April 1901. This opera had its libretto by Basil Hood. Sullivan had composed some of the music and the rest was by Edward German. *The Emerald Isle* continued until 9 November 201 for a total of 205 performances. Partway through the run Helen passed the management to William Greet who became manager for *Ib and Little Christina, Merrie England* and *A Princess of Kensington* which closed on 16 May 1903. The Savoy then remained dark until 10 February 1904 when it reopened under the management of Edward Laurillard with *The Love Birds* by Raymond Roze and Percy Greenbank. It starred George Grossmith Junior (GG's son), who later became Laurillard's partner in production of cinema films.

---

2. *The Diaries of John McConnell Black*, Vol 3, Investigator Press, South Australia, pages 197–200

17

The end of the operas & marriage to Stanley Boulter

Information about Helen's life and feelings after the death of Richard D'Oyly Carte is to be found in the diary of her brother, John McConnell Black.[1] There is also news about her marriage to Stanley Carr Boulter, and what he said when he courted her.

> 19 April 1901 The letter to mother from Helen dated 1 March (before D'Oyly Carte's death) says they could not possibly have come out one year ago unless he had abandoned all his enterprise (hotel and "big scheme") and lost his £60,000 savings which were invested in the "big scheme".
>
> 5 June 1901 We have had two or three letters from Helen since D'Oyly Carte's death. She seems very broken-hearted about it all. She does not fix any exact time for coming out as she says she must first obtain probate of the will and pay out various legacies etc. This letter started with news of the easing of the drought in John's part of Australia. At the beginning of May John reported that there had been horrible weather, nothing but heat and drought. Conditions improved on 5 June – "It is pouring tonight. A little over one inch of rain fell on Adelaide." The drought clearly had an adverse effect on John's income, and it may be that some of his concerns when he heard that Helen was marrying again might be caused by his belief that there would be less money for Helen's family in Australia.

1. *The Diaries of John McConnell Black*, Vol 3, Investigator Press, South Australia, pages 197-200

6 July 1901 Poor Helen seems very unhappy, judging from her recent letters. She speaks of herself as 'a thing hacked in two, and the wound aches more as time goes.' Says toward the end of the letter dated 1 May 'I will not attempt to tell you all the legal and other difficulties I have had in closing up my affairs – and the awful number of things I have had to think of in trying to provide for old and now feeble servants – for fear of forgetting someone. There are many pensioners for whom I wish to bank sums of money and for some I am buying annuities. You know that, like yourself, I only consider money as a trust to be used for the benefit of others and that is all I wish to do with anything that comes to me beyond my own old savings which suffice for my needs.'

She is selling and giving away all her furniture and household goods. Weybridge, the island in the Thames where D'Oyly had built a beautiful home goes to Rupert. Helen seemed to think she may sail this month.

1 August 1901 Helen's last letter (27 June) says that she has got rid of the Savoy Theatre altogether. It belongs to a company now. She has moved into Beaufort Buildings, which is part of the Savoy Hotel. Weybridge (on the Thames) has been sold to Rupert Carte, and she could not let 4 Adelphi Terrace to a private tenant and could not

D'OYLE CARTE'S ISLAND. THAMES. WEYBRIDGE.

(I think) let it to a club. – she has only got rid of it by paying £1,000 as rent for the two years the lease has still got to run. All the old papers, band parts etc have been taken over to the new offices. D'Oyly Carte's yacht and steam launch have been sold. With regard to the D'Oyly Carte company Helen writes as follows 'The Operas mean that I have personally bought up out of the estate all the Gilbert and Sullivan operas for four years and I am making a settlement of them for the benefit of our old staff who will run them, taking the fees and who will thus, I hope, make a little capital fund, if they save it to go against bad times.' She hopes in a week or two after the Palace Theatre mortgage has been settled to be able to distribute the estate and appoint someone to finish up.

Summer 1901 was a low point in Helen's life and a very low point in the future of the operas. She did not expect any revenue for more than four years. In fact, she must have renewed the arrangement in summer 1905, and this made possible the two repertory seasons which ran at the Savoy from December 1906 to March 1909.

John's diary continues to provide information about Helen. She had decided to revive a Gilbert and Sullivan opera that had been received enthusiastically when it was first presented on the Savoy Theatre stage.

25 January 1902. Helen has brought out *Iolanthe* at the Savoy Theatre[2] for the present lessee and writes more cheerfully about it. It does not look as if she is coming out here in any hurry although it will soon be a year since Mr Carte died. Mother takes it very philosophically.

31 March 1902. Mother brought down a curious letter from Helen yesterday, speaking of how she has always been accustomed to work for some man and under the direction of a man and going on to say that she has an old and dear friend of hers and D'Oyly's who would be glad if she would work with him, but that those sort of connections are not recognised by the world and are out of the question. It will be strange indeed if it ends in her marrying again after being in such despair for months. Mother wondered if the

2. The lords are from the first production of Iolanthe. The illustration comes from the supplement to *Play Pictorial* 209 (Tilly of Bloomsbury), edited by Sullivan's nephew B.V. Findon.

friend is W. S. Gilbert. He is still active although Sir Arthur Sullivan is dead.

5 April 1902. A letter arrived from Helen today, giving more particulars about her proposed marriage and justifying its propriety. She has been very unhappy – thought of taking her own life at the end of November – this old friend of D'Oyly's and herself came and

MR. DURWARD LELY.   MR. RUTLAND BARRINGTON.
"Iolanthe."

very soon offered her marriage. He is now pressing it. She did not give his name but says he is a lawyer and now, chiefly, a director and chairman of various companies. He has been a widower for about six years, lives in the country some 20 miles from London, and has three sons and four daughters. Helen asked me to show her letter to mother. She wrote most of it in the train while returning from Manchester to London. No rain of any use has fallen yet – if there is any coming it is all before us. I forgot to add that if Helen marries this gentleman it is doubtful if she can come out as he is desirous of marrying soon and it is questionable if he would make such a long journey with her.

This would have been Helen's last chance to see her mother. In the previous years, there had been no opportunities because Carte needed her help with the operas, or the hotel, or both.

The gentleman's name was Stanley Carr Boulter. He was born on 29 May 1852, so he was 17 days younger than Helen. He was educated at Clare College, Cambridge and decided on a legal career. He was called to the Bar in 1879. He quickly built up his reputation in London, and became editor of the Law Reports in *The Times*. As a barrister he worked on commercial and financial civil cases. He also undertook criminal cases, but these were generally concerned with fraud and breaches of bankruptcy laws. From 1885 onwards he was sufficiently eminent to appear before the Court of Appeal. In 1889, Boulter turned his energies to finance. He was a founder of the Law Debenture Corporation in 1889, and

remained Chairman until his death in 1917. He was also chairman of the Imperial Colonial Finance and Agency Corporation, and the New Investment Company. _The Times_ called him "one of the leading representatives of the great Trust Companies." Nobody was better than Mr. Boulter at handling a difficult meeting of shareholders, and restoring confidence. The financing of theatrical ventures has never been free from risk and bankruptcy courts in the early 1900s seemed to have been full of failed theatres and managements.

The Law Debenture Corporation was securely founded by April 1900, when Helen felt that she and Richard could not come out to Australia. The reason why Richard had to stay in London was that Boulter was in the process of raising funds for expansion of the Savoy Hotel. Boulter became vice-chairman of the Savoy Hotel group. The Law Development Corporation became one of Britain's top 350 companies.

Boulter was active in politics. He began as a Liberal, but disagreed with Gladstone over Irish home rule. He stood as a Liberal Unionist in the general election of 1886, but he was not elected. He moved towards the Conservative party, particularly in matters affecting the scope and strength of the British Empire. In social matters he remained a Liberal, and he advocated public assistance for working men wishing to buy their own homes. This policy would have appealed to Alexis in _The Sorcerer_. It must also have appealed to Helen.

Stanley Carr Boulter was the son of John Boulter of Frimley, Surrey. Boulter first married Edith née Anderson. There were three sons and four daughters of the marriage Edith died in 1896. So Helen was marrying into a full and lively family. We shall see in the next chapter that Boulter's children were active admirers of the D'Oyly Carte Company. Boulter's career, with its emphasis on law and accountancy may make him sound rather stuffy. The photograph of him in fancy dress suggests a lighter side.

Stanley Carr Boulter married Helen on 25 April 1902. They married in the fashionable church of St Martins in the Fields. The church is in Trafalgar Square, and no doubt they could look up to Nelson on his column as they came out of the church.

John McConnell Black's diary on 6 July 1902 has a sad entry:

Dear mother died at twenty five past six in the morning. She is lying in her room at Bellyett so peaceful and still and past all worry. Alice spent the night there and got up early with a feeling she was wanted. She found Miss Bethune (the nurse) supporting mother's head. She asked for some milk and water to drink. Alice handed it to her, and soon after drinking it she passed away very quickly and quietly, probably from a spasm of the heart. Alice said that mother had two or three hours' sleep after a sleeping draught and that when she woke she spoke nicely to her, more like her old self. She called the nurse Helen all through the night.

Mr. Stanley Boulter in court dress.
At a fancy dress ball at the Savoy Hotel

18

The revivals – comebacks for the operas & for Helen

Four years after the death of Richard D'Oyly Carte it must have seemed that Helen's participation in the operas was finished. In March 1905 Helen was laid up in the Savoy Hotel with pulmonary arthritis. It took a full year for her to return to normal working.

The end of 1906 saw a dramatic recovery in Helen's health. The tonic that she took was that she took charge of the two Repertory Seasons of Gilbert and Sullivan at the Savoy Theatre. *The Yeomen of the Guard* opened the first season. Helen showed herself to be fighting fit, managing a recalcitrant member of the cast. Here is an extract from letter to Rowland Williams Esq, 200 Vauxhall Bridge Road; SW. Williams had absented himself from the second of two photograph sessions.

> "Although under the agreements no salary is payable for the nights on which the Theatre may be closed, it has been my custom voluntarily to pay salary for the day on which the Dress Rehearsal occurs, in consideration of the fact that usually also the photographs are taken that day, and that it makes a somewhat long and tiring rehearsal; and I also provide refreshments for the Company. Under the circumstances I look to all the artists to behave well and loyally. I think you will understand that under the circumstances, and in fairness to the others, I should not feel justified in treating you the same way as those who stayed until the work was completed".

A handwritten addition says "It always distresses me when these things occur." This is pure Helen: Rowland Williams was Second

Citizen in that production of *The Yeomen of the Guard*. He never appeared in any D'Oyly Carte production again.

Helen planned to present *The Mikado* as the last opera in the First Repertory Season. Britain was about to welcome Prince Fushimi, Crown Prince of Japan. By 13 April 1907, Helen received intimations from high circles that *The Mikado* was not acceptable to the modern Japanese. So when the final opera of the first season opened on 11 June, it was with *Iolanthe*, not *The Mikado*. The intimations came from the Lord Chamberlain's office. The Lord Chamberlain, Charles Robert Spencer, later the sixth Earl Spencer, was the great grandfather of Diana, Princess of Wales.

Helen campaigned vigorously and skillfully against the removal of *The Mikado* from its prime position at the end of the First Repertory Season. She wrote letters of protest to several British newspapers and I particularly treasure an interview she gave to the *Dublin Observer*.

MIKADO VETO – PROPOSED PETITION TO PRINCE FUSHIMI – NO WITHDRAWALS IN THE PROVINCES – DEFIANT SHEFFIELD – STATEMENT BY MRS D'OYLY CARTE

The latest development against the prohibition of The Mikado is the organisation of a petition to Prince Fushimi who arrives tomorrow on a visit to the King. Mrs D'Oyly Carte has already received an immense budget of letters from correspondents who express their willingness to sign a memorial to the Japanese Prince. It is proposed to ask him formally whether he has any objection to *The Mikado* and, if not, whether he would be prepared to make representations to the Lord Chamberlain through the Japanese Embassy.

A representative of *The Observer* yesterday inquired of Mrs D'Oyly Carte if she could account for the interference of the Lord Chamberlain. She replied: 'The whole thing is inexplicable to me. The Press is full of disclaimers, both official and unofficial, of the idea that the opera can give offence to their country.

Helen wrote to *The Times*, complaining about the unfairness of the situation. She said that *The Mikado* was currently was currently making three times as much revenue as any of the other Gilbert and Sullivan operas.

In modern times, the situation is frequently referred to as a ban. The Lord Chamberlain's office never imposed a ban. Faced with a ban, any Member of Parliament or of the House of Lords could ask for an explanation why a ban had been imposed.

In 1907 Gilbert gave evidence to a parliamentary committee. He was cross-examined by Lord Newton:

"What occurred in the case of The Mikado?"

Gilbert replied:

"As far as I know, it was this. I was informed that the Lord Chamberlain had forbidden the production of *The Mikado* on the ground that it might give offence to our Japanese allies. I was not communicated with by the Lord Chamberlain, there was no preliminary correspondence. There was some feeling afterwards he simply took my property and laid an embargo upon it. Subsequently I had an interview with Lord Althorp. The Censor, I understand, had nothing whatever to do with the matter. "

Within a month of the battles over the staging of *The Mikado* and after a wait of many years, Gilbert was called to Buckingham Palace to be knighted by King Edward VII on 30 June 1907. The huge popular acclaim awarded to Helen's season of revivals may well have jogged the pen of the King's advisers. Gilbert would have enjoyed the fact that *Iolanthe* that was playing at the time. Of all the Savoy operas *Iolanthe* did most to satirise the House of Lords.

Helen had the last word in this season of skirmishes. The Savoy season ended on 24 August. The performance opened at 4.00 pm, and went on until 11.00 pm, with a one and a half hour break for dinner. To the astonishment of the audience, an extra scene was played. As soon as the audience heard the introductory music, wild demonstrations of delight broke out. Louie René as Katisha and C.H. Workman as Ko-Ko played their scene from Act II of *The Mikado*. Putting the scene into that first Last Night of the London season was a real coup de théâtre by Helen. And she wrote to *The Times* on 23 August outlining her plan to open the next Savoy season with *The Mikado*.

Last Nights of London seasons became highlights of London seasons for ever after that. They often changed in content and character. Rupert D'Oyly Carte used his first Last Night to end the 1919 to 1920 season when he returned from war service. I was present at the last First Night at the Adelphi Theatre on 27 February 1982. I am sorry to report that, unlike Helen's first Last Night, there was no dinner lasting one and a half hours.

There was no let or hindrance to the opera after 1907. Helen included *The Mikado* in the Second Repertory Season of 1908 to 1909 in those two Repertory Seasons; Helen brought the operas back with style and imagination. She re-ignited memories of golden days with the old favourites. Rutland Barrington had not appeared at the Savoy since 1896. In the Second Repertory Season he played in all six operas. The photograph of Helen with Barrington dates from summer 1908. She looks frail.

Helen made another very significant contribution to the future of the operas. The period during which Gilbert assigned the rights to perform them ran out in 1910, and needed to be renewed. Gilbert was not feeling friendly towards the Savoy Theatre management. Just before Christmas 1909, C. H. Workman replaced the girl singing Princess Selene, in Gilbert's opera *Fallen Fairies*. The fairy who fell (or was pushed out) was none other than Nancy McIntosh, adopted daughter[1] of (by then) Sir William and Lady Gilbert. Gilbert's fury was huge. Once again, Helen made good use of her tact, charm and friendship. Once again she got Sir William Gilbert to sign 'any blessed thing' that she chose. The quotation comes from Act II of *The Gondoliers*:

> When every blessed thing you hold
> Is made of silver, or of gold,
> You long for simple pewter.

The Boulter family enjoyed the revivals. Within six months of the start of the first season, Stanley Boulter held a party for Savoy performers at Boulter's home Garston Park, Godstone. The first photograph overleaf shows the group with Boulter's eldest son Cyril Boulter and his wife. The second photograph shows a different Boulter son in the same place. Both wanted to be in the picture.

---

1. In fact, Nancy McIntosh as an adult was too old to be legally adopted.

Mrs D'Oyly Carte entertains the Savoy Opera Company at Garston Park, Godstone

The names, reading from left to right, are: back row, (standing) – Messrs Richard Andean, Hancock, Tom Redmond, Frank Wilson, Mrs Russell, Messrs Moyle, Charles H. Workman, J.W. Beckwith (Business Manager), Albert James (Stage Manager), Stanley Carr Boulter, Harold Wilde, John Clulow. Miss Morrison, Leo Sheffield, "Mrs Dorothy 'Freckles' Sheffield, Francis Cowley Burnand and François Cellier

Middle row (sitting) – Miss Clara Dow, Mrs Bessi Workman, Mrs Helen D'Oyly Carte, Miss Louie René, Miss Jessie Rose, Lady Dorothy D'Oyly Carte, Mr Rupert D'Oyly Carte

Front row, (sitting) – Mr Cyril Boulter, Mrs Cyril Boulter, Miss Norah Macleod, Miss Beatrice Meredith, Henry A. Lytton, Miss Violet Frampton, Miss Marie Wilson and Miss Ruby Gray

More thoughts about Garston Park

This photograph is similar to the one opposite and was clearly shot on the same day, but there are some significant differences. The opposite page shows 30 people; this page shows only 27. The main differences are in the Boulter family.

At the end of the front row are Mr R. Boulter (wearing a dark jacket and Mrs Boulter, In the same place in the other picture are Cyril Boulter and Mrs Boulter, The dark rosette on the front of her dress is the same as that worn by the lady in the other picture. She may be a daughter of Stanley Carr Boulter. The date is May-June 1907, based on the fact that Sydney Granville has not yet gone to Australia. Rupert D'Oyly Carte, extreme right in the middle row, is wearing a moustache.

It interesting that Helen's name is headlined as Mrs D'Oyly Carte, she had been married to Stanley Carr Boulter for more than five years, and she was at a party arranged by the Boulter family. Nonetheless, her professional identity was Mrs D'Oyly Carte.

133

This is another photograph taken at the time of the Repertory seasons, almost certainly during the first season. Gilbert was knighted by Edward VII on 17 July 1907, so it is not certain that he had become Sir William Gilbert at the time of the photograph. It may even be a gathering to celebrate his knighthood.

From left to right: soprano Clara Dow, Lucy (or Lady) Gilbert, contralto Louie René, Helen and Nancy McIntosh, Helen looks to be enjoying herself and well aware of what is going on. Gilbert's wife looks as though she does not share her husband's enthusiasm for being photographed with other ladies.

It may be unkind to notice that Clara Dow, supreme for her Victorian blonde chocolate box beauty is not quite so spectacular off-stage.

Grateful thanks to Melvyn Tarran for his generous permission to publish the picture here. It is one of the many G&S rarities which he has in his collection at Oak Hall Manor in the beautiful Sussex countryside.

When the Second Repertory Season ended C. H. Workman still held the lease of the Savoy Theatre. He produced Eden & Somerville's *The Mountaineers* (September–November 1909), appearing as Pierre; Gilbert & German's *Fallen Fairies* (December 1909–January 1910), appearing as Lutin; *Two Merry Monarchs* (March–April 1910), appearing as Rolandyl; and *Orpheus* (April–May 1910). *The Era* complimented him as both for his acting and his exquisite refinement of the mounting and dressing of the piece. "Mr C. H. Workman as Rolandyl played with his usual alertness and drollery. His never-flagging vivacity and his remarkable resources in the way of business and gesture kept things going wonderfully." *Two Merry Monarchs* only ran until 23 April. With it ended Workman's time as Manager.

He planned an imaginative coup. Helen D'Oyly Carte had purchased the acting rights in the operas in 1905 from Gilbert and from Herbert Sullivan, Sir Arthur Sullivan's nephew and heir. Workman found out those rights were about to lapse. He asked Herbert Sullivan to ask Gilbert whether he would consider an offer from Workman. Gilbert wrote to Workman on 22 June 1910:

"I do not intend to waste any epithets on you – you can easily supply them yourself. It is enough to say that no consideration of any kind would induce me to have dealings with a man of your stamp."

Gilbert sold the rights to Helen for £5,000 for five more years. He probably stipulated that Workman would not be allowed to work again anywhere in Britain in his operas. Workman never did. He appeared on 10th September 1910 in Oscar Straus's *The Chocolate Soldier*, based on George Bernard Shaw's *Arms and the Man*. It ran at the Lyric for 500 performances. Constance Drever was Nadina, and Elsie Spain played Mascha. Workman appeared in *Nightbirds* (the early English title of *Die Fledermaus*), from 30 December 1911. He emigrated to Australia in 1914.

An extra irony is that he was preceded to Australia by Charles Walenn, who had been a touring comedian from 1891 to 1903 and was called back to the touring company when Workman went to the First Repertory Season. In April 1907 Walenn was defended by a note from touring Business Manager Henry Bellamy to the Savoy – "Referring to Mr Walenn being a little indistinct – especially in patter – he has had two or three (front) false teeth lately." By the time Workman reached Australia, Walenn had settled there. So had his front teeth. Walenn became principal comedian in the main Williamson Company.

The success of the revival seasons meant that more people than ever wanted to stay at the Savoy Hotel. So Helen's final contribution was made in bricks, mortar and scaffolding. *The Builder* reported:[2]

> "Structural works of a particularly interesting character are now in progress at the Victoria Embankment part of the Savoy Hotel. Briefly stated, the works include the virtual abolition of the main wall hitherto constituting the façade and the construction of a new wall about 8 feet 6 inches nearer to the river so as to increase the size of all the bedrooms and to provide bath, lavatory and other sanitary conveniences in either one or two small rooms directly accessible from each apartment. In addition, the old mansard storey[3] over the entire block is being enclosed by an upward extension of the outer walls, and above it a new mansard storey is under construction."

The conversion of the old mansard storey and the storey above created space for 30 suites of additional rooms. By covering in the courtyard behind the embankment block, a banqueting room capable of seating 500 people was installed.

2. *The Builder*, Savoy Hotel Extension 10 September 1910, pages 292-294
3. A four-sided <u>gambrel</u>-style <u>hip roof</u> characterized by two slopes on each of its sides with the lower slope more vertical than the upper, punctured by dormer windows to create additional habitable space

A particular feature of the new extension was that the hotel now had a swimming pool. Helen would have been delighted to provide this novel facility, which she may have noticed when she stayed in hotels in North America. Stanley Boulter may have used his contacts in London's financial world to provide some of the money that the new Savoy Hotel extension and amenities would require.

19

The death of Helen D'Oyly Carte

Helen died on the evening of Monday 5 May 1913, at Savoy Court, which was part of the Savoy Hotel. She was a week short of her 61st birthday. Her death certificate gives the cause of death as cerebral hemorrhage, cardiac failure and bronchitis. Her body, like Gilbert's two years earlier, was cremated at Golders Green. The funeral service, in accordance with her expressed wishes, was of the simplest character and only attended by near relatives.

Helen had been in poor health for several years. She was visited by her brother Alfred and his wife. Before sailing on 29th September 1911 he received a letter from Stanley Boulter.

> "My dear little wife ruptured a small vessel in the head. I am afraid it was brought on by her continued paroxysm of coughing which at times was quite distressing to her. She lost the power of the right arm and her face and speech were affected. I am glad to say there has been a slight improvement almost daily since but it is a slow one and the doctors lead one to expect only a very gradual recovery. We have kept her very quiet since the attack with, I am happy to find, good results. She is in no pain and very comfortable and peaceful."[1]

Helen's life had undoubtedly been shortened by the hours she had spent on the detail of organising the activities of the Company. The theatrical world paid its own special tribute towards the end

---

1.   The Diaries of John McConnell Black, Volume III

of her life. The managers of all the provincial and suburban theatres asked Helen to accept a manifestation of their regard, which was in vellum and signed by 25 managers.

Helen suffered a stroke in January 1913. Dame Bridget remembered seeing Helen in her last days. "I was four years old and saw her at the Savoy Hotel. She was very ill."

John McConnell Black's diary contains a letter sent by Stanley Boulter on 30 January 1913:

> "I am grieved to tell you that dear Helen had another seizure on Tuesday last which has weakened her very much. The limbs on the right side have now lost their power, as well as those on the left side. She is, I fear in a very serious condition. She retains her consciousness and takes her food fairly well. Her temperature is good, so is her pulse. I am now in a most depressed condition, for my hopes of her recovery are of the most slender. But my joy is still great that the dear little invalid is spared to me and that she is able to recognize me and understand what one says to her."

The Times obituary placed great emphasis on Helen's personal qualities[2].

> "Exceptional business ability and great energy were combined with a very retiring disposition and stored in a very slight and fragile frame. Early hardships had given Mrs D'Oyly Carte an insight into the needs of those in her employ, and her real sympathy and open-handedness were rewarded, not only by the award of Order of Merit, which the King conferred on her last year, but by the affection of all who worked with her".

The theatrical world greatly regretted Helen's death. Here is a piece from *The Stage* magazine[3] in London:

> "The passing away of Mrs D'Oyly Carte removes from the active theatre sphere the last of the old-time lady managers which numbered the honorable names of Mrs Sara Lane of the Britannia, Mrs Chas Rice of Bradford (aunt of Mr John Hare), Mrs Ellen Nye Chart of Brighton, Mrs J.W. White of Huddersfield and many others. We still have with us Mrs

---

2. *The Times*, 6 May 1913
3. The Music Box by James M. Glover. *The Stage* London 15 May 1913, page 23

Stoll, the mother of Mr Oswald Stoll, who nightly practises her mascotte duties in the box office of the Coliseum."

Helen's role as one of the four partners in the success of the Gilbert and Sullivan operas was recognised in Parliament by Lord Denham in the House of Lords on 1 April 1998.[4]

> Lord Denham rose to ask Her Majesty's Government what measures, if any, they could take to help to save the D'Oyly Carte Opera Company. The noble Lord said: My Lords, on 23rd March 1875, 123 years ago last Monday, *Trial by Jury*, the first successful collaboration between William Gilbert, the librettist, and Arthur Sullivan, the composer, opened at the Royalty Theatre in London. Both were brilliant but neither could achieve anything like his best except in partnership with the other. The only trouble was that they quarreled so much that they were unable to work together without the mediation of the equally brilliant impresario, Richard D'Oyly Carte. *Trial by Jury* was followed over the next 21 years by *The Sorcerer* and 11 other light operas. The Savoy Theatre was completed by Richard D'Oyly Carte in 1881, principally for the presentation of the works of Gilbert and Sullivan. Richard himself died in 1901 and the company was taken over, first by his widow Helen, and on her death by Rupert, his son.
>
> Helen was among the first of a special generation of lady managers in the theatre. Within two years of finishing her studies at London University in 1874, she decided to turn her attention to a career in the theatre. She committed herself to that career throughout her life. Her success in management made it possible for other women to succeed in the theatrical profession.

4. *Hansard*, Debate of 01 April 1998 volume 588 cc353–74

20

Helen's legacies

Helen's last will and testament is dated 11 March 1909. She added a codicil on 11 March 1910. The probate figure for Helen's estate was £117,670 5s 1d. Considering that the net amount she received in Richard D'Oyly Carte's will was about £75,000, and that there had been a slump both in hotel shares and theatrical audiences, Helen had managed her money well. Her brothers John and Alfred had each been left £5000. Her money helped John publish his definitive study, *The Flora of South Australia*.

John had been intensely suspicious of Stanley Carr Boulter. His diary entry dated 5 July 1913 says that it was probably all fiction that Boulter was a wealthy financier and he simply married Helen for her money... He wrote: "Well, now he has got it."

Helen left bequests to other members of her father's and mother's families, and to staff of the D'Oyly Carte Company and the Savoy Hotel. The residue went to her husband Stanley Carr Boulter.

Helen had been aware that the value of her shares had gone down and this may have been why she added a codicil in March 1910. On 7 July 1910, Helen wrote to John.

"Hotel shares have gone from bad to worse on the Government threats. Our 7% £10 preference shares which were reckoned at, I think, £14 each for Estate Duty when I distributed the estate in 1901 are quoted at £6/3/4, ordinary shares are below £5, and so on. The theatre is still unlet, and since the death of the King there is quite a slump in theatres. We (Rupert and I) have to meet the outgoings unless the buccaneer shareholders foreclose, so the outlook

is not very cheerful. I still hope we may get a sound tenant if we take quite a low rent (enough to pay the interest)".

The range of people to whom Helen had left cash or Savoy Hotel shares is fascinating. To George Reeves Smith, she left ten 5% debentures of £100 each. His father, also named George Reeves Smith, had been the manager of the Brighton Aquarium. He was the man to whom Helen had sent offers of singers and speakers in Chapter 5. The same bequest went to François Cellier, Musical Director of Carte's London and touring companies for thirty years. She left twenty 5% debentures of £100 each to her old friend Fred Billington. The codicil to Helen's will, dated 11 March 1910, says that she has already made some additional payments to Billington and so the number of debentures was reduced from twenty to five.

Helen also left £500 to Harry Bellamy, who was employed as the acting manager of the opera company. Henry Ernest Bellamy had first joined E Company in 1888 where he sang the named parts of Samuel in *The Pirates of Penzance* and Pish Tush in *The Mikado*. He later took the tenor role of Luiz in *The Gondoliers*. From 1894 he became Business Manager of various D'Oyly Carte companies, and he took this position in the Secondary Revival Season (1908–9) at the

Savoy. He continued as D'Oyly Carte's Business Manager all the way through to his retirement in March 1920, Helen left £200 to Annie Russell, D'Oyly Carte's rehearsal pianist at the Savoy.

Throughout the latter years of her life, Helen supported charities, with emphasis on actors' charities, sick children's charities and her great love of dogs. She left 50 debentures to the Actors' Benevolent Fund. High on the list of bequests in her will was £200 to the Royal Society for the Prevention of Cruelty to Animals. She also left ten 5% debentures of £100 each to the Temporary Home for Lost and Starving Dogs. This charity is now Battersea Dogs and Cats Home. The legacy to the Lost and Starving Dogs was revoked in a codicil on 11 March 1910. It may be that Helen had reduced her confidence in Savoy debentures. On the other hand the bequest to François Cellier was increased from five debentures to ten.

Helen made other donations to good causes during her lifetime. In 1900, when the leading theatrical managers proposed to present her with her portrait, she asked that all the money collected might be used instead to fund a cot in the Children's Hospital Great Ormond Street, for the benefit of the Actors' Benevolent Society.

She received a framed tribute from 25 managers of suburban and provincial theatres as a token of their esteem. This illuminated address was still on display in the D'Oyly Carte offices when I went there as editor of *The Savoyard* magazine in the early 1980s. It may have been passed to Albert Truelove. The 25 signatories were for the most part managers of West End theatres. They included Beerbohm Tree and John Martin Harvey.

There was another presentation to Helen upon her retirement from London management on 19 November 1910. The committee consisted of Sir Charles Wyndham, Sir H. Beerbohm Tree, George Alexander, George Edwardes and Edward Terry. The intention was to commission a portrait. However, Helen's health caused considerable delay and she informed the committee, with much regret, that she finds it quite impossible to sit for her portrait. Instead she asked for the money collected to be applied for the benefit of the Children's Convalescent Home of the Victoria Hospital.[1] A cot named in perpetuity – Mrs D'Oyly Carte presentation cot. The right of naming successive occupants of the cot was to be placed at the disposal of the Actors' Benevolent Fund. The secretary of the Fund was W. S. Fladgate, of, 2 Craig's Court.

---

1. The Convalescent Home of the Victoria Hospital for Children at Chelsea was opened in 1892 by Princess Louise.

There were three echoes of Helen's early career. Wyndham had sent her to act in the provincial tour of *The Great Divorce Case*. George Edwardes was Box Office Manager at the Opéra Comique when Helen joined Carte's team in 1876. And Craig's Court was where the team was working. There was yet another connection. The Royal Victoria Hospital for Sick Children was opened in 1866. A group of Chelsea residents raised funds to provide a hospital for 'poor afflicted children'. The first medical officer was Sir William Jenner, physician to Queen Victoria. Within the grounds was the White House, built as a studio for James McNeill Whistler.

As we have seen in Chapter 8, Whistler gave advice about décor when Richard and Helen moved into their flat in Adelphi Terrace and he was their friend for years afterwards.

To sum up, I shall quote George Edwardes, Guv'nor of the Gaiety Theatre, who worked with Helen so closely in the Carte office at the start of her theatrical career

"A more wonderful woman it has not been my lot to know. It was my privilege to work with her under D'Oyly Carte for quite a considerable time, and I never ceased to marvel at her extraordinary energy, her inexhaustible activity. She labored day and night. The whole foundation of the Savoy business rested upon her. She settled the tours, engaged the artists, and did everything short of producing. And if any trouble arose, it was Helen Lenoir, or as she subsequently became, Mrs Carte, who put it right.

You could not be with her a minute without feeling the extraordinary magnetism of her presence. Everybody loved her. Sullivan, Gilbert, myself – the entire staff of the theatre."

This is the last letter from Helen that I have seen. It is appropriate that Helen quotes from *The Gondoliers*, the last opera from a golden age.

Index

University College School 30
Utopia Ltd 51, 104–5, 107–8

The Vicar of Bray 104

Walpole, Hugh 8–9
Warwick, Giulia, 24
Whistler, J McNeill 58, 66–8, 74

The Wicked World 19
Wigtown 6–8, 11
Wilde, Oscar 47, 58–9, 66–7
Williams, Rowland 128–9
Wilson, Mozart 116
Workman, C H 130–1, 135

The Yeomen of the Guard 51, 82, 84, 128